ARIZONA SHOWDOWN

ARIZONA SHOWDOWN

A WESTERN QUARTET

LES SAVAGE, JR.

SAGEBRUSH
Large Print Westerns

First published in Great Britain by ISIS Publishing Ltd.
First published in the United States by Five Star

Published in Large Print 2011 by ISIS Publishing Ltd.,
7 Centremead, Osney Mead, Oxford OX2 0ES
United Kingdom
by arrangement with
Golden West Literary Agency

British Library Cataloguing in Publication Data
Savage, Les.
    Arizona showdown.
    1. Western stories.
    2. Large type books.
    I. Title
    813.5'4–dc22

ISBN 978–0–7531–8760–9 (pb)

Printed and bound in Great Britain by
T. J. International Ltd., Padstow, Cornwall

Five Star Publishing, a part of Gale, Cengage Learning.

CONTENTS

Night Ride

Although in retrospect it is difficult to explain, in 1950, the same year that Fiction House would close down *Action Stories*, which it had begun publishing in 1921, and *Lariat Story Magazine* that had appeared under this name for the first time with the August, 1925 issue, the company launched a new magazine titled *Indian Stories* that continued publication for three issues before being discontinued. Les Savage, Jr. sold this story to *Action Stories* and was paid for it on April 15, 1949. It did not appear in that magazine but instead in the inaugural issue of *Indian Stories* (Summer, 1950) under the title "Hostage-Maid of Massacre Mesa."

CHAPTER
ONE

The young brave and his white captive picked their way along the ledge high above the yawning gorge to the cliff house. There was a heavily armed guard squatting by the door, and he rose to pull aside the sheepskin covering. The inside was dark and smelled of raw wool and the crumbled pottery of the ancient people who had lived here long before the Navajos came. The girl was barely visible, standing against the wall, stiff with fear.

Iris Ballantine's hair was dimly visible in the gloom, gold as honey. The dusk turned her breasts to half moons, swelling against the calico of her dress and the lapels of her blue military cloak, whitened by alkali. Her voice trembled when she spoke.

"Who are you? Why am I here?"

"You are at Cañon de Chelly," the tall savage figure said. "I am Nah-wah-ti Tahnee. The traders call me Quick Arrow."

She licked her lips. "Why was I brought here?"

"The Long Knives' general has captured our war chief, Hosteen Tso. We thought if we had the Long Knife general's daughter as hostage, he would not be inclined to keep our war chief."

"How did you know I'd be on that stage?" she said thinly.

The Indian studied her, seeing pride and courage slowly overcoming the fear. "We have men in Santa Fé," he said, stroking the silver guard on his wrist. "We heard that the Long Knives' chief's daughter was coming to Fort Wingate from the East. So we ambushed the stage. We mean to hold you till your father frees our war chief."

"Father will never do it," Iris Ballantine said thinly. "He'll come in here and wipe you out."

Tahnee shook his head. He spoke English perfectly although with a certain up-and-down cadence derived from the Navajo. "The Long Knives' general knows that would mean your death. We already have word from the white trader at Yellow House that a rider from Fort Wingate is waiting there with terms. *Hatali* thought you would want to send a message."

Her eyes flashed to the second man in the room. "*Hatali?*"

"It means medicine man," Tahnee said coldly. "This is *Hatali* Anaji. He commands the tribe with the war chief gone."

Iris turned back to Tahnee again, narrow-eyed. He made a tall form in the gloom, lean-hipped and wide-shouldered, wearing a pair of use-softened rawhide leggings, a sheepskin vest. The bare flesh of his muscular shoulders gleamed like polished bronze. There was a narrow refinement to his head; the eyes were set deep beneath black brows; there was a sculptured strength to his lips.

4

"I never heard an Indian speak such good English," she said.

The tall brave showed no pleasure, no emotion at all. He said: "I don't know where I learned it. When they found me at Kintyel, I could speak it."

"Kintyel? Isn't that the ruins north of Fort Wingate?"

He nodded. "The Mexicans know it as Pueblo Bonito. Now," he said sharply, drawing himself up, "if you wish to send a message to your father, I'll take it."

She seemed to steady herself against the wall. "Tell my father that, if exchanging me for your war chief means starting a war, I would rather that he marched in here and wiped you out."

Tahnee stiffened, surprised at the vindictiveness of her voice. "The return of our chief will not mean war. All we ask is to be left in peace. His capture was a mistake. He was at Yellow House signing a treaty when the young warriors in his party got out of hand and tried to kill your father. The general thought it had been a trap and took our war chief in reprisal."

"*Shighe,*" *Hatali* said. "My son." The old man put his hand on Tahnee's arm, drawing him toward the door, speaking in Navajo. "She would not say this if she knew us better. She is frightened. It is time for you to go. Peshlikai is at his forge in the cañon. You will take him with you."

"Silversmith?" Tahnee asked. "Must I take him?"

They pushed out through the door and past the guard hunkered before the door. "Silversmith has great influence with the trader at Yellow House," *Hatali* said. "You will need him if anything goes wrong."

5

Tahnee shook his head. "He's a member of the *Nahnest teh'zhih* clan. I've never trusted them."

"Perhaps the woman from which the *Nahnest teh'zhih* originated was a Zuñi," *Hatali* said. "But that was so long ago we have almost forgotten where the name of the clan came from. The Zuñi-Navajo clan is as loyal as one of pure blood."

"I'm not so sure," Tahnee said. "I have seen Silversmith talk with the Zuñis in their own language. A man does not do that unless he has had much contact with them. And you know the Zuñis would be happy to see our power broken here."

Hatali chuckled softly. "I have heard the same words spoken against you because you know the language of the whites. But I am sure Silversmith is as loyal a Navajo as you."

Tahnee said no more, following the old man down into the cañon. *Hatali* Anaji had been his guardian and mentor through the days of his youth, and was now his closest friend. The old man had a leonine mane of white hair, falling to the shoulders, and wore a cloak made from a red Chimayo blanket that covered him to the ankles, flapping constantly at his beaded moccasins.

They reached the bottom, where the sheer rock walls tumbled off into talus slopes and finally became the broad floor of the cañon, patched with the cultivated fields of the various clans and the countless hogans of mud-chinked logs.

This cañon had been the home of the Navajos for over 150 years. It had been the Spaniards who had originally driven them into Cañon de Chelly. This great

6

gash in the high plateaus of northern Arizona, guarded at each end by such narrow entrances, had been so impregnable that none of the enemy tribes had ever attempted to storm it. Only once had the Spaniards succeeded in entering. That had been in 1805, and what happened to them gave the tributary Cañon of Death its name.

Now, in 1850, another conqueror had come. Fort Wingate had been established in New Mexico Territory, and the tribes outside Cañon de Chelly were beginning to fall to the whites. Already there were many Zuñi scouts in the pay of the Americans, and other Pueblo Indians had been brought under white rule. War had not yet officially been declared between the Navajos and the Americans, but there had been many skirmishes between the young braves and scouting parties of white troops. This was one of the reasons Hosteen Tso, the war chief, had gone to Yellow House to sign the treaty.

Tahnee and the old medicine man made their way past the winking fires and the singing squaws and groups of eating men till they came in sight of Peshlikai, Silversmith, squatting over his goatskin bellows.

He was heavy-muscled for an Indian, with the sweat shining like oil on his coppery skin. He had a broad face, with cheek bones pointed up so obliquely that it gave his eyes a deep, Oriental slant. His Apache war *botas*, folded over at the knee, were caked with dust blown up by the bellows, and his buckskin leggings were held up by a belt of immense silver *conchas* that he had made from Mexican pesos.

"*Ahalani,* Peshlikai," *Hatali* said.

Silversmith glanced up, then rose, giving them the universal greeting. "*Ahalani, Hatali.*" His obsidian eyes moved to Tahnee. "Is the *yei* from Kintyel going with us to Yellow House?"

The old medicine man's bloodless lips drew thin. "You and Tahnee are going on a mission together. I want you to forget the hate that has lain between you. You will cease to mock him."

Silversmith's slant-eyes widened. "But I do not mock. Because of his exploits many of the people say that Tahnee is a *yei,* a true god, sent down to help us in our battle against the whites."

Hatali shook his head. "You know it is not true, Silversmith. We only named Tahnee after the Beggar Boy of Kintyel because when we found him the signs were so close to the story in the Bead Chant. We haven't time to talk now. Get your horses."

Tahnee turned away to go and get his pony where it was tethered to the hogan he and *Hatali* shared. When the Spaniards had first conquered the Southwest, they had done it on just such barbs as this beast, hammer-headed and short-backed, with a deep infusion of Arab in its heavy throttle and dense bones. Silversmith joined Tahnee, mounted on a hairy pinto. They bid good bye to the old medicine man, and the people crowded along their path to see them off.

Near the eastern end of Cañon del Muerto, they picked up Gontzo. His name meant Big Knee, from the swollen knee he had gotten in a fight with the Zuñis. He was a sour veteran of thirty-five with a face scarred from a hundred battles. His buffalo-hide shield, traded from the Comanches, made a muted *clatter* against his horse as he rode up.

"The Zuñis should usurp our power when we do things like this," he complained. "In the old days we would have risen up and killed all the whites within a thousand miles."

"The whites are not like our old enemies," Tahnee said. "No matter how many are killed, more keep coming. We must make peace with them if we wish to remain a great people."

Silversmith's eyes tilted up at the corners. "Attend closely, Gontzo, a *yei* has just spoken."

Tahnee brought his barb over against the pinto with a jerk of the rawhide reins, eyes blazing. "You not only offend the gods, Silversmith. You offend me. You will not call me a *yei* again."

Silversmith's eyes tilted higher with his sly grin. "But you are a *yei*, Tahnee. Why else should they name you after the Beggar Boy of Kintyel? It all happened just like the myth in the Bead Chant. They found you as a child with the most beautiful sand painting they ever saw. You told them of White Head Chief and the Kisani. And all the birds were seen. Long-legged Crane and Great Blue Crane . . ."

"*Tchindi*," muttered Tahnee. "You have mocked me enough."

Silversmith pulled his horse to a halt. "Did you hear him call me a devil, Gontzo?"

"Silversmith," Gontzo said. "We cannot afford trouble now."

But Silversmith had already gripped Tahnee's wrist, pulling him closer. "You will ask my forgiveness, Tahnee. I do not wish to have the curse of such a name remaining in the air."

Tahnee's voice was barely audible. "Let go of my hand."

Silversmith's teeth showed. "And if I don't?"

Tahnee's whole body stiffened, but before he could go any further, Gontzo had ridden in on the other side of Silversmith, taking his arm. "Peshlikai, I said we cannot afford to have trouble now!"

A strange expression filled Silversmith's broad face. He settled heavily into the saddle, staring at Tahnee. Then his hand slid off Tahnee's arm, and he turned his eyes to Gontzo. Something passed between the two men.

"You are right, Big Knee," he said. He glanced sullenly back to Tahnee. "This can wait."

Tahnee stared at the man a moment longer, white-lipped with anger. Then he put the heels to his halted horse and it bolted ahead. They crossed the Rio Puerco and rode the night out in the wastelands beyond, passing through mesquite forests putrid with the summer crop of beans decaying on the ground. And as Tahnee's anger cooled, he found the picture of the girl coming to his mind. There had been more than one Navajo girl who attracted him, but none as deeply as this white woman. For some reason he could not forget

10

her. The image of her kept recurring to him all the way to Yellow House.

With dawn they reached Zuñi country, and scouted the mesas carefully for the enemy before sitting down to breakfast of cold mutton and dried corn. Then they pushed on, passing through Yeitso's Bones, the bizarre country of toppled, broken columns that the Navajos believed to be the bones of an ancient giant killed by their war god.

After that they turned north again and rode into the mountains. The horses began to shine with sweat as they pulled up the jagged slopes robed with juniper and scrub oak. Then the sun flamed over the peaks and shone red as blood on sandstone cliffs ahead of them. They came in sight of Brian Clay's trading post, a cluster of adobe buildings like toy blocks on a tawny carpet.

A group of men filtered from the door before the three Navajos reached the yellow buildings. Brian Clay was in the lead. He was the biggest man in the group, with immense shoulders and a square keg of a belly swelling at his red wool shirt. He wore a pair of greasy Army blues with the yellow cavalry stripe torn off their seams. He had a shaggy mane of red hair, a great furling beard, and brows so dense and lowering they almost hid his eyes.

With him were his two men. Pepper walked to the hitch rack and leaned indolently against it, chewing one of the chiles that gave him his name. He had once belonged to the Navajos but had tried to become a white man. The result seemed to be nothing but all the vices of both races. His gaunt, starved face was pitted with pocks, his eyes were yellow-tinged and bleary with drink, his hollow chest and deep cough revealed a body wracked with the consumption so many Indians who took up the white man's ways seemed to contract.

The second man, Yeats, leaned casually against the yellow wall of the adobe trading post, thumbs tucked into his gun belt that supported the holsters of twin Walker Colts.

Clay greeted the Indians with a broad grin, waving his hairy hand at the Army officer beside him. "*Ahalani*, brothers. This is Lieutenant George Sherwin, from Fort Wingate. The Navajo on the left is Big Knee, Lieutenant. The one in the middle is Silversmith. The third one is Tahnee. He speaks our lingo."

The lieutenant nodded his narrow blond head perfunctorily, calculating each man with a cold blue glance. The rigid line of his slender body made Tahnee think of a tempered sword blade. His uniform had apparently been impeccable when he started from Fort Wingate, but there was a layer of alkali whitening the gauntlets folded over his belt and the spurred jackboots on his feet. Tahnee stepped down from his horse and faced the lieutenant.

"Clay sent word you would meet us and make terms."

Sherwin's sun-bleached brows lifted in surprise. "I never saw an Indian who spoke English like that."

Pepper chuckled. "Claims he no got white blood, Lieutenant, but look at this curl to hair. *Tchindi*, I think he's white renegade or somethings hides out in Chelly . . ."

"Shut up," Clay said roughly. "I'm tired of you running off at the mouth."

Tahnee saw resentment flame for a moment in Pepper's face. But Clay turned a blistering glance on him and Pepper's eyes fluttered and dropped to the ground. Silversmith and Gontzo watched him with open contempt in their faces. It was the attitude all Indians held for members of their race who tried to become white. Over by the wall, Yeats rolled a cigarette, watching it all from enigmatic eyes.

"We didn't come here to blow words to the wind," Tahnee said. "We came to make a trade . . . this girl for our war chief."

Sherwin's sunburned face grew ruddier. "Very well," he said stiffly. "Here are the terms. You are to bring Iris Ballantine here next Saturday at high noon. Your party is limited to five. Four of them are to stop a quarter mile from the buildings here. Only one will accompany Iris this far. We in turn only have five men in our party, and only one of us will accompany your war chief to these buildings."

Tahnee translated to Silversmith and Gontzo, and they agreed. When the other minor details were finished, Clay made an expansive gesture with his hand.

"Now that the business is over, let's all go in and have a drink to pledge our good faith. You understand, Silversmith. *Toghlepai.*"

Silversmith nodded his understanding, licking his lips expectantly, but Tahnee caught his arm. "This is

13

not time for drinking," he said in Navajo. "We must keep clear heads."

"Let him have drink," Pepper said. "How often you get stuff like Clay give? I never taste thing like last time you come. One drink and them five bucks so drunk they try for shoot them whole American Army . . ."

Clay swung around with one arm outstretched, the back of his hand smashing Pepper across the mouth. It knocked him off the hitch rack and slammed him against the wall of the yellow house so hard he was stunned. He slid down the wall to a ludicrous sitting position, staring stupidly up at Clay.

"I told you to shut up," Clay said thickly. "Next time you start gabbing, I'm going to bust your neck."

Pepper wiped slack, wet lips, squinting in pain. He shook his head dazedly, climbing to his feet with great difficulty. He tried to meet Clay's eyes again, but his glance fell, and he stood against the wall like a whipped dog. Clay jerked his head at Silversmith, and turned inside. Silversmith shook off Tahnee's hand.

"I drink when I please," he said sullenly, following the trader.

"Verily." Gontzo grinned, limping after Silversmith. "The white man's *toghlepai* is much more potent than ours."

He spat on the ground at Pepper's feet as he passed him, and then disappeared through the door. Tahnee watched them go, hot with anger. Then he realized how closely the lieutenant was staring at him, and turned to the man.

14

Sherwin took the gauntlets from his belt, beating the dust out against his legs. There was an odd, strained look to his face. Over by the wall, Yeats finished his cigarette, flipped the butt aside, and turned in the door. Pepper scrambled for the butt. Then he, too, went inside, holding the remains of the cigarette with the thumb and forefingers of both hands and sucking on it avidly. Sherwin was still staring at Tahnee, and finally spoke.

"How is she?" he asked. His voice sounded tight.

Tahnee stared at him. "You know her well?"

Lieutenant Sherwin slipped on one glove with a vicious tug. "Yes," he said. "Very well."

"Oh." Tahnee almost whispered it. "That well."

"Yes." Sherwin yanked on his other glove, voice breaking sharply. "That well." He took a step toward Tahnee, something wild in his eyes. "I asked you how Iris was."

"Safe," the tall young brave said. "Unharmed."

Sherwin's weight came forward on his feet till his face was not a foot from the Indian's. "You'd better keep her that way," he said. His voice trembled faintly. "If anything happens to her, Tahnee, I swear I'll hunt you down and kill you myself."

He continued to stare with those hot bright eyes for another moment. Then he wheeled to his horse, throwing the reins back over its head and whipping up into the saddle. He clapped his heels to its flanks and put it into a dead run off across the sandy flats. Tahnee stared after him, face sober and thoughtful. He could understand Iris Ballantine inspiring that kind of feeling in a man. He could understand it too well.

Finally the voices from within broke into his thoughts. He could hear Silversmith laughing huskily, repeating something in English that Clay had said.

"Gold." Silversmith pronounced the word haltingly. "Dollars."

"That's right." Clay chuckled. "Gold dollars. Thousands of them. Millions of them. You must have a fortune in that damn' cañon. You Navajos have been raiding along the border for two hundred years now and nobody's ever been in Chelly to take it from you . . ."

He broke off as Tahnee entered. "We are often confused with the Apaches," Tahnee told him. "They are the ones who raided the Spanish gold trains in the early days. We only fought when we were threatened. Most of our loot has been sheep and horses we won in war from neighboring tribes."

"How would you know about our treasure?" sneered Silversmith in Navajo. He had a half-empty bottle of whiskey in his hand, and his eyes shone with drunken malevolence. "Only the *hatalis* know where it is hidden."

Tahnee looked at him in surprise. "You understand what we are talking about? You seem to have learned much English."

A guilty look flashed through Silversmith's eyes, then he snorted defiantly. "I can understand enough. I think Clay is right. There is a treasure. *Hatali* Anaji and his

16

old men have been keeping it from us. It is the young men who should have it."

"You are drunk," Tahnee said. "It's time to go."

"I do not want to go," Silversmith said.

"Enough of this," Tahnee said angrily, yanking the bottle from his hand and hurling it against the wall.

Before the tinkling *crash* had ceased, a rough hand spun Tahnee around and he found himself facing Brian Clay. "You'll pay for that," the man said.

"Not after what Pepper said," Tahnee told him. "You got those braves drunk last time for a purpose. The Long Knives' general wouldn't have taken our war chief if it hadn't been for that. Are you trying to bring war between your people and mine?"

"The hell I am!" shouted Clay thickly. He caught Tahnee's shoulder and bulled him back into the wall. "No filthy sheepeatin' scalp-lifter is going to come in my place and . . ."

Face rigid with rage, the tall Navajo tore loose with a jerk and caught Clay's arm, swinging the trader around. The man's own impetus carried him, staggering, across the room. He crashed into the barrel holding up one end of the counter. It skidded away from him and his sliding feet carried him, falling, beneath the planks of the counter as they came down, canned goods and sacks of flour and sugar tumbling about his head.

Tahnee saw Yeats come away from the wall, pulling at his Walker Colts. The smooth-moving brave took a running jump and hit Yeats feet first in the stomach as the Colts came free. Both guns went off at the floor as Yeats staggered backward into the wall.

The grinning Navajo fell away from the man and hit the floor on his back. He saw Pepper darting toward a corner of the room as he rolled over onto hands and knees. Raising up off his hands, he yanked his short bow and an arrow from the case on his back, notching the shaft and drawing down on the ration Indian. Pepper brought up sharply in the corner, huddling there in terror.

"Please," he whimpered, reverting to Navajo. "I meant nothing, Tahnee, I meant nothing." From the corner of his eyes, Tahnee saw Yeats pawing for one of the guns he had dropped. He swung around till the arrow bore on the dour man. Yeats halted, staring, wide-eyed, down the shaft. Clay was crawling dazedly from beneath the counter.

"Shoot him, Yeats," he snarled thickly. "Shoot him."

"Better not try," Pepper hissed, wiping the spittle off his slack lips. "They say he get four arrows out of bow before first one hit target."

"Five arrows," Tahnee corrected with that unIndian grin of his. He got to his feet, bow still drawn. "And you'd better stay gopher-still till we ride 'less you want me to prove it."

CHAPTER
TWO

The three Navajos got back to Cañon de Chelly the next morning. Tahnee told *Hatali* the terms, and then went up to tell the girl.

Little daylight could get into the cave houses up on the cliff, so they had lighted a small fire in the *estufa* in the corner of the room. The white woman was sitting on one of the old green-gold *bayeta* blankets in the corner when Tahnee entered, the firelight turning her hair to newly minted gold. She had removed her cloak, and he could not keep his eyes from the ripe curves of her body in its flowered calico.

"The terms have been set," he said. "We take you back Saturday." He saw her eyes light up with relief. "Lieutenant Sherwin will be there. He'll meet you," he continued, observing the effect of this closely. A flush sent its delicate tint through her cheeks and she dropped her eyes.

"You like him much?" he asked.

"I . . . I don't know. I met him at West Point. He was very gallant."

"He said he'd kill me with his bare hands if anything happened to you."

She turned her eyes up in a startled way. Then she tried to laugh. It sounded embarrassed. "That does sound awful, doesn't it?"

He studied her. "I'm glad you don't feel about him as he does about you."

"What do you mean?"

He dropped down beside her, sitting on the mat. "Would it make any difference if I was white?"

"Any difference in what?"

"In how you felt toward me."

Her underlip seemed to pout with her understanding. "It's the first time an Indian has ever made love to me," she said half jokingly.

"I'm serious," he said.

"Are you?"

Their faces were so close that her breath fanned his cheeks. He stared at her lip, drawn by its ripe pout. He had seen Mexicans do it in the *cantinas* down in Tucson. He had seen a white man do it. But he had never done it himself. Yet it seemed the most natural thing in the world. She caught at his arm, trying to twist away. But he pressed her backward with the weight of his body. Her lips were like moist satin against his. When he finally pulled away, he was breathing heavily. She stared at him with wide, startled eyes.

"I should have stopped you," she whispered. "I started to ... but ..." She trailed off, a wonder growing in her eyes. She shook her head suddenly and pulled away with a *hissing* rustle of calico and stood up

20

sharply, walking to the *estufa* in the corner, standing there with her back to him staring into the flames.

"Does it bother you so much that you were kissed by an Indian?" he asked, rising.

She wheeled back, staring at his face, as if seeking something there. "Somehow," she said, "when you were kissing me, I didn't think of you as an Indian, or as a white. Just a man . . . kissing me."

The tall brave stared intently at her face, drinking in its loveliness, his shoulders dragged down by the growing realization of how futile this was. He took a heavy breath.

"I shouldn't have done it, I guess," he said. "After you go back to Fort Wingate, I will probably never see you again. None of the Navajos from Cañon de Chelly is even allowed within sight of the fort. An Indian . . ."

"But that's it." She came toward him swiftly, putting her hand on his arm. "There's something about you, Tahnee. The way you speak English. The color of your eyes, your hair. Are you really an Indian?"

He shook his head, smiling ruefully. "I have been asked that so many times. Sit down and finish your breakfast, while I tell you about it."

She sat down, looking up in wonderment. He turned toward the fire, beginning the story. First he told her the myth that was contained in their Bead Chant. It was of *Nah-wah-ti Tah-nee*, the Beggar Boy of Kintyel. According to the Navajo religion, it had happened long ago, when the ruins of Kintyel were a great and populous city, and the Beggar Boy had been a pariah, subsisting on scraps outside its walls. He had saved the two sons of the eagle chief from the cruel conquerors who lived within the city, and for this was transported to Skyland, and taught how to make sand paintings by the White Head, the War Eagle. When the Beggar Boy returned to earth again, he called all the people together at Round-Top Hill, above Kintyel, and made the first sand painting, attended by Long-Legged Crane and Blue Crane and the other four birds that made up the sacred colors of the sand paintings.

"When the Navajos found me," Tahnee explained, "they say I was sitting in the middle of a beautiful sand painting, half-finished, and I spoke to them in their own language of White Head and Skyland and the Kisani who used to inhabit Kintyel. On the way back to Cañon de Chelly, all six of the sacred birds were seen. All this seemed so much like the original myth that they named me after the Beggar Boy."

She was watching him intently. "It's uncanny," she said.

"You do not laugh?" he asked.

"Why should I?"

"Many whites think our religion silly."

"I realize much of it is symbolism. It can't be judged by what it seems to be on the surface." She frowned. "How old were you when they found you?"

"About five."

"Do you remember anything before they found you at Kintyel?"

He shook his head. "I remember people. But they're like shadows. I remember a hogan like none of our

22

hogans. It seems to be made of adobe bricks. And there is a man with a black hat."

"There." She rose swiftly, eyes sparkling with excitement. "Don't you see? If you had spoken English until you were five, and had been brought into contact with whites enough after that to retain the language, you'd still speak it fluently. And the man in the hat?"

He shook his head. "I have talked of it so many times with *Hatali*. He says the man with the hat is only a dream." He stared at the ground. "How can I know, when even their finding me is like a dream. These are my people, Iris. I feel it. I would have it no other way."

She came close to him again, speaking softly. "Perhaps I can help you. Father has connections . . ."

He pulled away, sick at heart. "Why fool ourselves? I am an Indian. You are white. There is no meeting ground. It is better that we part . . . that I don't see you till Saturday."

He turned and pushed through the sheepskin covering the door. It seemed very dark outside. From the bottom of the cañon, 500 feet below, the fires winked like 1,000 fireflies in the night.

He was still standing on the ledge, a few feet from the door, when *Hatali* came laboriously up the trail. The old medicine man peered into Tahnee's face as if he could see the trouble there even in this darkness.

"You have had a long journey," he said. "*Tah'tsay* would purify your body."

"I don't feel like the sweat bath now," Tahnee told him, staring down at the cañon. "*Hatali*, when they found me out there at Kintyel, in the sand drawing, with the birds about me, did I speak our language?"

Hatali peered into his face. "Of course."

"I have some kind of memory about you teaching me the words. *Es-shee,* and *Teehay-ah.*"

"You have been talking with the white woman," *Hatali* said. "It is not only your body which needs to be purified, it is your mind. You do need *tah'tsay.*"

They went down the trail and across the fields and through the villages in the bottom of the cañon till they reached the sandstone obelisks guarding the end of Monument Cañon and they went deeply into this tributary gorge until they reached the sweat house. It was a small conical structure of sticks and adobe beside the running waters of a creek.

Tahnee stripped naked while *Hatali* built a fire to heat the rocks. Tahnee stepped in and the rocks were thrust in behind him and the door was closed tightly. Squatting in the growing heat with the sweat beginning to roll off his glistening bronze body, he started the sweat-house chant.

Nayenezrani will spread the earth
With beautiful flowers.
An everlasting world and a peaceful world . . .

He sang the first four verses and pushed his way out to plunge himself in the cold waters of the stream, and then went back in. The shock of sudden change and the great heat and the weakness of sweating was making

him giddy by the time he came to the part about First
Woman.

> She put it down, she put it down, First Woman put
> it down . . .

He began to have visions. He saw Johano-ai, the Sun
God, riding his Turquoise Horse across the sky. He saw
Nayenezrani slaying Yeitso and toppling his bones over
the land. He saw First Woman bending gently over him.
Only it wasn't First Woman. It was Iris Ballantine.
When he finally finished the chant and staggered out,
weak and giddy, *Hatali* Anaji was waiting for him.

"Did you have dreams?" the old man asked, rubbing
him off with clean sand.

"I dreamed of the gods," Tahnee said. "But I
dreamed of the white girl, too."

Hatali stopped rubbing him with the sand and stood
there for a long time, staring off into the distance. "It is
plain the girl has planted something in your mind that
cannot be erased," he said. "Perhaps she is not at fault.
This was bound to happen sooner or later. It is time
that you know the truth. I was afraid to tell you before.
You had become so invaluable to us. I was afraid you
would leave us if you knew."

He let a handful of sand run out between his fingers,
watching it. "I was the one who found you first at the
ruins of Kintyel," he said at last. "I was a young *hatali*
then. I had gone there to fast and dream of the gods.
My four days of fasting were up and a party of young
men was due to come and take me back to the cañon,

when I found you. I knew they would think you were a child of our enemies, and probably kill you, or at least leave you there to die. I have never believed in such cruelty. I quickly made as much of the sand painting as I could, and taught you how to say White Head and Skyland and Kisani, and a few other words of Navajo. Then I hid on the other side of the ruin and left you playing in the sand painting. When the young men came, they thought they were the first to find you."

Tahnee stared at him. "The omens saved my life."

Hatali nodded. "You spoke the words I had taught you, the way a child will repeat a thing. I joined the party afterward. They did not actually see all the six birds in the Bead Chant. They saw a mockingbird and that started it. I began pointing to other birds in the sky, and the power of suggestion took care of the rest. When we got to Cañon de Chelly, the young men had such a wonderful story to tell of your discovery that many people still believe you are really the Beggar Boy, returned to help us."

"Then who am I, really?" Tahnee asked.

"Many years after finding you, I met a Zuñi chief who had a gold watch taken from a white trader he had killed. The trader's wife and son had also been killed in the fight. But there was a second child who got away. From what I could gather, it had happened near Kintyel, within a day of when I found you."

Tahnee stared at him, eyes wide and blank. It was like a sharp, sickening blow to the stomach, after so many years of believing he was an Indian.

26

Hatali nodded sadly. "You must have been that trader's child. You wandered through the desert to Kintyel. You are really white." He studied the young man's face for a long time. "I could have kept it from you longer, I suppose. But I can see how you feel about the girl. Her questions would have started you questioning. It is better that you have the complete truth. And now that you know it, will you leave us?"

Tahnee turned to stare off down the cañon, brow knotted by a frown. "I don't know," he whispered. "I don't know."

CHAPTER
THREE

They started before dawn. They started with a few
mongrel dogs howling and yapping at their heels and
an awakened baby crying in a hogan. A pitifully small
party for such an important mission. Five Navajos and
the girl, each with a spare horse, setting out down the
great, chill cañon with the ancient walls frowning down
and the dawn turning the sky beyond the gates to milk.

Hatali Anaji rode as far as the end of Cañon del
Muerto with them and gave them a last benediction,
and they rode out of their stronghold singing *hozhoni*
songs. Tahnee rode in the lead, beside the girl. Behind
came Silversmith and Gontzo and Hosteen Yasih, the
head man of the Bead Clan, and one they called
Nahkai because his mother had been Mexican. Tahnee
rode without talking much to Iris, his mind still in a
turmoil from what *Hatali* had told him the other day.

Late in the afternoon they reached Yeitso's Bones.
The Indians would have ridden on, but Iris was tiring,
and Tahnee made them stop. While the Indians made
camp, Iris went over to one of the immense, crumbling
columns.

"This looks just like wood," she said. "Only it's hard
as rock. Are those petrified trees?"

28

"They are the Bones of *Yeitso*, the greatest of all evil gods," Tahnee told her. "This is where our war god killed him. *Yeitso*'s blood covered the country with blackness south of where your Fort Wingate now stands."

"The lava beds," she said. "Dad wrote me about them."

He smiled. "I'll show you *Yeitso*'s hand."

Silversmith looked up from where he was building a fire. "Do not wander too far, *yei*," he said.

Tahnee turned back to see a secretive smile tilting the man's eyes up slyly. Thin-lipped, Tahnee turned to lead Iris into the maze of great fallen trees, some broken into round sections, others still intact, their serrated surface glittering in faithful reproduction of bark. The ground was covered inches deep with a vivid mosaic made up from spalls of creamy chalcedony and mottled jasper and black and blue and red agates that had been chipped off the trees through the ages.

They were out of sight of the camp when Tahnee pointed out *Yeitso*'s hand. The main trunk and branches of the petrified tree had fallen so that they spread out in the exact shape of a hand and its fingers, broken at the joints into great disks. Iris leaned against one of these, looking at Tahnee. In the dusk, her face had a satiny texture.

"When will we reach Yellow House?" she asked.

"A little before noon tomorrow," he said.

Her voice was throaty with sadness. "Such a short time."

He came close. "Does it really mean so much to you?"

"I don't know," she murmured, staring up at him, searching his face for something. "I've been trying to find out. I couldn't forget you, after you left, the other night."

"I couldn't forget you, either."

"Tahnee" — she reached out to grasp his arm — "it doesn't have to end. I could come to meet you at the trading post."

"What would that mean? Sneaking off for a few minutes together! What would your father do if he found out?"

Her shoulders dropped. "Send me home, I suppose." Her underlip formed a stubborn shape. "It's cruel. We don't ask much. Just to be together."

"Just how much do you want to be together?"

She stared up at him for what seemed a long time, strange emotions shuttling across her face. "If we only had more time, Tahnee," she said at last. "How can a person tell, in only one day?"

"Would it help if I was a white man?"

He saw hope leap into her eyes. He knew a great impulse to tell her what he had found out, to show her there was a chance. Before he could speak, he thought he heard a shout, and turned. The fallen trees cut them off from sight of camp. Then he heard the sound. It was a small *crunching* sound. It came from his left.

Quickly he snaked one foot behind the girl's knee, putting all his weight against her at the same time. Her leg buckled, and with a gasp she went down. He tried to roll off instead of falling on top of her, reaching for his short bow where it was slung on his back. He had it out and strung when Yeats appeared suddenly, climbing through one of the breaks in a giant tree trunk, one gun out. With his first sight of Tahnee, Yeats fired.

But Tahnee was still rolling, and the bullet chipped an agate spall off the petrified tree behind him. Then he had the first arrow notched and it left his bow with a *swishing* whip of air. It struck Yeats in the shoulder before he could fire again, and carried him over backward so that the second arrow went above him as he fell.

Tahnee was up on his knees, meaning to rush for the man, when he heard more noise behind him and tried to whirl. But a hurtling weight struck him on the back, smashing him forward to the ground, and something hit his head with a great explosion of pain. His face dug into the layer of agate chips when he hit the ground.

He rolled over, deeply dazed by the blow, face cut and bleeding. He felt someone on top of him, felt the shift of weight as the man set himself to strike again. Tahnee opened his eyes to see the war club descending, Silversmith's twisted face behind it.

Tahnee rolled aside from the blow. The head of the club scraped past his ear and sunk into the chips. He caught at Silversmith's arm with one hand, driving a blow at the man with the other. It sunk into Silversmith's belly. He saw the man's face contort with pain. He gathered all his forces into one titanic effort to roll the man off. He felt himself going over, coming up on top. He saw Silversmith's arm bending again, tried to catch it and stop the blow.

But Silversmith twisted beneath him, bringing a knee up. With a sick gasp, Tahnee bent over the man. At the same time, that war club came up again. It smashed against the side of his head, knocking him off Silversmith. He tried to save himself. Could not. The club hit him again. He heard Iris scream. He was falling into blackness. He knew nothing more.

CHAPTER
FOUR

Tahnee regained consciousness with the sun in his face. His head was filled with a throbbing pain. When he tried to open his eyes, it hurt so much he closed them again. He felt someone's hands on him. Water was forced between his lips. Finally he opened his eyes. Lieutenant George Sherwin was bent over him. The man's face was an alkali mask through which sweat had worn greasy grooves in the lines about the eyes and mouth. His voice sounded guttural and driven.

"Where is she? What happened?"

Sickly Tahnee tried to gather his thoughts. "Silversmith attacked me. Yeats, too."

"I don't believe you." Sherwin was shaking him, eyes red and feverish. "Where is she? Damn you, Tahnee, I told you what would happen if you harmed her."

"I had nothing to do with this," Tahnee said, struggling feebly to get out of the man's grasp. He shook his head dazedly. "I don't know why they didn't kill me."

Sherwin sat back on his hunkers, studying Tahnee closely, disbelief still turning his eyes wild. "All that blood, they probably thought you were already dead."

Tahnee reached back to feel his head caked with dried blood. He was weak and dizzy from the loss of it. "How did you get here?" he asked Sherwin.

"When you came to Yellow House to get the terms, Clay mentioned your route would be through the petrified trees," the lieutenant said. "I'd scouted this area and knew where the place was. When you didn't arrive on time today, I sent my men back to Wingate with your war chief and came hunting you." He had a cap-and-ball Colt in his hand, and jerked it up suddenly. He bent toward Tahnee and his voice was savage and bitter again. "Where is she? Damn you, Tahnee, I'll kill you."

Tahnee rolled over and sat up, leaning back against the serrated trunk of a great fallen tree. He stared dully at the gun, too sick to react. Finally he shook his head.

"Can't you understand, I didn't have anything to do with this? I wanted to bring her back. I wanted peace between your people and mine."

Sherwin settled back slowly, studying Tahnee's face. "Two of your men are dead at the fire," he said finally.

"Silversmith? Gontzo?"

"No. I never saw them before." Sherwin frowned at Tahnee. "Does that mean Silversmith is the one behind this? Why should he do it?"

"The only thing I can think of is that Silversmith is a Zuñi-Navajo," the tall brave said. "The Zuñis have long wanted our power overthrown. If the girl isn't returned, the Long Knife general will march against Cañon de Chelly. If he defeats the Navajos, the Zuñis will have a chance to become powerful again. Being part Zuñi,

34

Silversmith will be a famous warrior among them for having stolen the girl and brought about the downfall of the Navajos."

"Then how did Yeats get into it?"

"That must mean Brian Clay is in this, too," Tahnee said. "Yeats is Clay's man. Clay must have put this in Silversmith's mind the other day. Clay speaks a little Navajo, and Silversmith understands more English than I gave him credit for. They were talking of the treasure the Navajos are supposed to keep at Cañon de Chelly. It has long been legend in this land."

"What would that have to do with kidnapping Iris?"

Tahnee shook his head feebly. "Perhaps Clay has some idea that he can gain the treasure this way."

Something desperate entered Sherwin's face. "Can you ride?"

Tahnee drew a shaken breath. "I guess so."

"Let's go back to Yellow House."

CHAPTER
FIVE

The wind came down out of the spruce forests in the
peaks and swept the sand into great banners that furled
across the flats and broke and scattered against the
adobe walls of the buildings and settled to the ground
at their base to pile up like drifts of snow. The Army
horse stumbled doggedly down the long slope with the
wind plastering its tail across its rump and the two men
on its back huddled against each other, their eyes stung
almost shut by the constant battle with blown sand.
They approached the trading post from its blind rear
end, where the high adobe walls of the corrals cut off
vision from the windows. Sherwin dismounted and
walked around the front while Tahnee climbed from the
back of the horse to the top of the corral wall and
dropped inside amid the burros and half dozen ponies
huddled together.

He found an inside gate that led him across a second
smaller adobe pen to the rear door of the trading post.
It was shut but not locked. He opened it and stepped
inside, finding himself in a long hallway. He heard a
pounding on the front door, and Clay's voice.

"Who is it?"

From outside came the lieutenant's muffled answer: "Sherwin. Let me in."

Tahnee was at the other end of the hall, looking into the main part of the trading post, when Clay opened the door. A blast of sand followed the lieutenant in, spattering across the dirt floor, and Clay leaned against the door to close it.

"You find anything?"

"Plenty," Sherwin said. "Silversmith has kidnapped Iris, and Yeats was involved. That means you're involved, Clay."

Standing in the shadowy hallway, where Clay could not see him, Tahnee saw surprise cross the trader's face. Then something sly entered his eyes, almost hidden beneath their shaggy red brows. He stepped back to the counter, hooking his elbows on it and leaning indolently against the planks.

"Now how do you figger that, Lieutenant?"

Sherwin took a vicious step after him, grabbing the front of his shirt. "I don't figure it. I know it. What are you mixed up in this for, Clay? Where is she? You know, damn you, you know."

"Let go me, shave tail," Clay said, "or Yeats will blow off the top of your head."

Sherwin let his hands slide off, turning sharply. Tahnee saw it now, too. The stairway came down from a room at the rear. It was in the deep shadows on the far side of the room, half hidden by bolts of cloth and shelves of tinned goods. Yeats had come down so quietly even Tahnee had not been aware of him till now. His right arm was in a sling and bandaging around that

37

shoulder beneath the torn, bloody coat gave it a bulky look. In his left hand he held a gun.

Clay chuckled indulgently. "It's too bad you found out so much, Sherwin. Now you'll have to die on a tour of duty. 'Way out there in the mountains. I won't even know about it till the Army finds your body or some Zuñi shows up at Wingate ten years from now wearing your boots."

Sherwin glanced at him, face pale. "You'll never get away with this, Clay."

"They'll never trace it to me."

"I don't mean killing me," Sherwin said. "I mean the girl. What in hell do you hope to gain by taking her away like this?"

"A million dollars maybe."

Sherwin stared at him. "You talking about the treasure they're supposed to have at Cañon de Chelly? That's a myth."

"I've got better informed sources than you, and they say it ain't."

"If you mean Silversmith, he's playing you for a sucker," Sherwin said. "Breaking the Navajo's power might make him a big man with the Zuñis, but it won't get you any million dollars. Silversmith just needed the help of your men to get the girl away from Tahnee . . ."

"That's a lie!" Clay came away from the counter, blood darkening his face. "Gontzo is already on the way to Chelly to tell the Navajos we have the girl. If they don't send as much gold as they can pack to Yellow House by the middle of next week, we do away with the girl. They know that will mean General Ballantine will

38

march on Chelly and wipe them out. They're not fools enough to bring that down on their heads. You'll see these rooms piled to the roof with Spanish doubloons . . ." He broke off, a sly smile twitching up one corner of his mouth. "Or maybe you won't." He took a step to one side, putting himself behind Sherwin. "Take care of him, Yeats."

Yeats had not yet seen Tahnee, standing in the black-shadowed hallway. The single-action hammer on the man's Walker Colt made a sharp *click* in the moment of silence. But Tahnee already had an arrow notched and the string back to his ear. The *swish* of the shaft came an instant after the *click* of the hammer. Yeats's mouth jerked open and he was slammed back against the wall and pinned there by the terrific force of the arrow. His gun went off at the roof in a deafening explosion, and then dropped from his hand. Clay wheeled toward Tahnee, surprise contorting his face.

Tahnee already had another arrow to his string, pointed at Clay. "Where is Iris Ballantine?" he asked.

Clay's face was the color of paste. He stared, wide-eyed, at the notched arrow, then turned toward Yeats, still pinned against the wall, dead mouth sagging open. Then he looked back at Tahnee. His throat twitched, and he spread his feet doggedly against the floor.

"You'll never find her if you kill me," he said thinly.

"We can beat it out of you," Sherwin said.

Tahnee studied Clay. If the man did not quail before the threat of an arrow, with the horrible example of Yeats still pinned to the wall, it was probable that he had the brute courage to take a beating without telling, either.

"I don't think that way will work," Tahnee told Sherwin. "Find some molasses."

Both Sherwin and Clay looked at him in surprise. Then Sherwin slowly turned and went behind the counter, rummaging beneath it till he found a jug of black-strap.

"There's an ant hill just around the corner of the building outside," Tahnee told him. "Start pouring out the molasses there and make a line to that soft earth about ten feet from the wall. You'll dig the hole, Clay. Find a shovel."

Tahnee saw the sweat start out on Clay's face, as the man understood. Tahnee jerked the drawn arrow at him, and he jumped as if burned. Then he wheeled, throat working faintly, and got a shovel. He went out after Sherwin and ahead of Tahnee. Sherwin found the ant hill and began to pour the molasses. Tahnee showed Clay where to dig. Clay sank the shovel in, then stopped, and stepped back.

"I won't dig," he said. "You can't make me."

Sherwin came to them, leaving a thick line of molasses behind him, and set down the jug. Already the ants were swarming out of the hill onto the trail of the viscid molasses.

"We'll dig then," Tahnee said. "Sherwin, hold your gun on him."

Tahnee put arrow and bow into the case on his back and took up the shovel. He went at it steadily, till the sweat began to pour from him. It was running off Clay's face, too.

"Was it you who found the man the Apaches had buried down by Tucson?" Tahnee asked Clay, stopping to rest. "The ants had eaten his eyes out, hadn't they? He wasn't dead, though. What did he say to you?"

"You won't do it," Clay said. His voice was hoarse.

Tahnee gave the shovel to Sherwin, and took his gun. "You're dead wrong, Clay," he said grimly. "The girl means more than our lives, to each of us. Sherwin is in love with her. My people will be wiped out unless we find her."

The wind whipped the sand against them in ragged streamers. Clay rubbed it irritably off his sweating face, blinking his eyes at Sherwin. The lieutenant dug without looking at the trader. The ants had reached their feet now, and were working at the molasses in a growing swarm.

"We don't have to stand Clay up in the hole, the way the Apaches do," Tahnee said. "Just deep enough for him to sit in."

Clay licked his lips, staring at the growing hole. His eyes held a yellowish tint. His cheeks seemed to have sunk in. Tahnee had seen fear do that to men before. He relieved Sherwin on the shovel. He did not know how much longer he could last. He was weak and sick from that blow on the head. His head was swimming and it was hard to breathe. But grimly he kept on. He could see how it was working into Clay, and he kept on. Finally they had it deep enough.

Tahnee dropped the shovel and pulled an extra bowstring from his arrow case. He stepped up to Clay with this strip of rawhide, trying to get behind the man. But Clay whirled and started fighting him. Sherwin stepped in behind Clay and clipped him with the gun barrel. Clay fell against Tahnee, sagged to his knees.

Sherwin held the man there while Tahnee lashed Clay's hands behind him with the bowstring. Then they dragged the semiconscious trader over to the hole, arranging him in a seated position. This way, his head was just above the ground level.

Tahnee began shoveling the dirt back in. Clay was half buried when he began to regain consciousness. He blinked his eyes, shook his head. Then he realized what they had done. Horror twisted his face and he fought to struggle out. Tahnee shoved him back in with a foot, throwing in more dirt till its weight held the tied man down. Clay's head jerked desperately to Sherwin.

"You won't let him do this, Lieutenant." His voice cracked. "You're a civilized man, you won't . . ."

"Shut up or I'll shoot you," Sherwin said.

Clay snapped his head back to Tahnee. "You can't do this. You're not all Indian. You must have some white in you somewhere. You can't do this, Tahnee . . ."

"It usually takes an Indian to stomach this," Tahnee told Sherwin. "He'll probably scream a lot. You can go back in the building if you want."

"You keep covering him," Sherwin said. "I'll pour the molasses on his head."

Clay made a strangled sound. He seemed to shrivel up. He looked at the huge red ants, busily working at the molasses not a foot away. A couple had started over to investigate him.

"All right." Clay could hardly control his voice. He looked like a little old man, huddled there in the hole. "They took her up to Pueblo Bonito."

Tahnee straightened up, staring at the man. Finally he said: "If you're lying, Clay, we'll come back and finish this job."

"I'm not lying," Clay said brokenly.

Tahnee dug the man out till he could untie his hands. Then he dropped the shovel and headed toward the corral. He saddled a horse for himself and ran all the other animals out ahead of him. Sherwin slung his Army saddle on a fresh animal and mounted up, turning the Army horse into the herd of free animals that they drove before them as they headed northward from Yellow House. Clay stood on the windswept flats behind them, a defeated figure in the fitful curtains of sand, watching them leave. Without a horse, he would be helpless to follow them. Before he was out of sight, Sherwin turned to Tahnee.

"One thing I'd like to know," he said. "Would you have gone through with it?"

Tahnee grinned ruefully, shaking his head. "I guess I'm not a very good Indian. I couldn't have done it."

CHAPTER
SIX

The country north of Yellow House was a high, flat land from which sandstone upthrusts leaped suddenly, to throw a jagged silhouette against the sky for half a mile and then to drop off just as suddenly into rough hills shaggy with clusters of stunted junipers. It was the Back-to-Back Month of the Navajos, white on top and green on the bottom, with snow glittering on the peaks of distant mountains, and grass growing in the valleys. Despite the greenery, a chill descended upon the land as the night grew near. They reached the tower-like Kinyai ruins, crossing the remains of an ancient irrigation canal, grown over with grass. Then they reached Chaco Cañon, and Kintyel. They halted on a rising height of land to stare down on the crumbling ruins the Mexicans knew as Pueblo Bonito. Tahnee stared at the ancient buildings with strange emotions. This was where *Hatali* Anaji had first found him. He had returned before, sometimes to fast and dream. But never before had he known what he knew now.

"It's a big ruin," he told Sherwin. "Hundreds of rooms. You had better circle around to the other side and keep them from escaping that way."

Sherwin studied Tahnee a moment, narrow-eyed. Then he wheeled his horse to circle the low ground, keeping to cover. Tahnee dismounted, taking his bow from the case and stringing it, pulling free an arrow. He worked within cover till he found the sign. It was of six horses, but the hoofs of three animals sank deeper than the others. That meant three ridden horses and three led. Clay had said Gontzo had gone to Cañon de Chelly to tell the Navajos. That would leave Pepper, Silversmith, and the girl.

At last, with dusk spreading a textured mantle over the ruins, Tahnee began to work toward the buildings. He reached the last cover of trees and brush, with 100 yards of open ground left to get across. Only an Indian could have done it without being seen. He crawled on his belly most of the way. He was caked with dust and running blood from myriad scratches by the time he reached the first stone wall. He halted here, listening, but there was no sound. Finally he found an opening and moved into the dark interior. Here was the same musty odor that clung to the cliff houses at Cañon de Chelly, an ancient odor that seemed to emanate from the crumbling artifacts of a long-dead race. He halted again and, while he was listening, realized that he could not use his bow. The darkness was like midnight. If he met them here, he could not shoot for fear of hitting Iris.

He slipped the bow and arrow back into his case, pulled his knife free. The blade was made from the lance tip of a Spanish lancer who had fallen in battle with the Navajos long ago; the handle was bone

45

wrapped in rawhide. He moved on through the fetid rooms, crunching through broken pottery, brushing the dust of ages from the walls. Then a voice from ahead stiffened him suddenly. It was Iris.

"Lieutenant, can you hear me? Silversmith says he'll kill me if you try to come in."

Tahnee realized they must have caught sight of Sherwin, trying to cross that open ground between the sandstone and the buildings. The lieutenant answered, his voice muffled and far away.

"Reason with him. Tell him I've got a whole squadron here. He hasn't got a chance."

"I can't talk that much with him. He only got this across by sign language and the few English words he knows. He's desperate, Lieutenant. He hasn't killed me so far because he wanted a lever to use against the Navajos. But now you've got him against the wall . . ."

Her voice broke off, as if she had been pulled back. Tahnee felt the breath gag in his throat. He could only guess what Silversmith would do now. Perhaps leave Pepper behind to hold off Sherwin and try to escape back this way with the girl.

"Iris!" called Sherwin. "Can you hear me? Stall him somehow. Give us a few minutes."

Iris did not answer. Then, from somewhere deep within the buildings, Tahnee heard the first faint whinny of a horse. It was cut off sharply, as if a hand had tightened the noseband. He reached an opening. The ghostly ruins rose all about him. He was looking out into a great, littered courtyard, empty as death. He heard the muffled stamp of a horse. It came from far back in the ruins. He found a hall and moved carefully down its dark length. The sweat made channels in the dust caking his body. Suddenly his foot struck something. It fell with a small *clatter*. He halted; there was dead silence for a moment. Then Silversmith called in a husky whisper.

"Gontzo, is that you?"

It was so close it startled Tahnee. He knew he would have to reach them before Silversmith realized it wasn't Gontzo. The girl's life hung in the balance. He broke into a dead run down the pitch-black hall. He heard Iris gasp; there was the sound of a sharp struggle.

"*Juthla hago ni!*" swore Silversmith in a great shout, and by that Tahnee knew he would kill Iris in the next instant. Still running, he heard her cry out. Then he went into them, hands pawing for the one he wanted. He felt calico rip beneath his fingers, and sensed that the girl was already falling. A blow struck him in the face, smashing him against the wall. Dazedly he realized it was Silversmith's stone war club.

He threw himself back, still fearful of using the knife, clawing for the man with his free hand. His fingers hooked into the immense silver *conchas* of a belt. He lunged with the knife. The war club struck him in the face, just as he felt his blade sink through flesh. He heard a sick gasp and didn't know whether it was Silversmith or himself.

All he could do was let his rush carry his body on into the man. Head spinning from the blow, blinded by his own blood, he felt Silversmith stagger back from his rushing body, and then fall, and they went down together.

They fell onto some steps and rolled over and over down these with the knife still in, the two reaching a lower half level. Silversmith threshed beneath Tahnee like a fish out of water, striking wildly with that club again. It struck Tahnee on the ribs, and he heard his own shout of pain. There was only the animal instinct to kill left in him. He pulled the knife free and struck again. He heard Silversmith gurgle, and his own body rocked to another blow by the war club.

He had one more burst left in him. Sprawled out on the man, drenched with sweat and blood, he pulled the blade free once more. The club smashed him in the face. With the last vestige of will, he drove home with the knife again. Silversmith stiffened, then went limp.

Tahnee did not know how long he lay there after that. Finally he heard someone whimpering, over in a corner.

"Tahnee," Pepper said. "I meant no harm, I meant no harm . . ."

It was a long time before Tahnee could speak. "Get out," he said feebly. "You aren't worth killing."

He heard a scurrying sound, like an escaping rat, and it was silent again. He tried to move, could not. Then he realized someone was kneeling beside him. Soft hands on his face. Iris.

With a great leap of joy, he realized Silversmith had not killed her. Sherwin began calling; Iris answered. In a moment the lieutenant joined them, and helped the girl get Tahnee into the open. Here they seated him against a wall; Sherwin got water from his canteen; Iris tore a strip from her dress and began to wash the blood off Tahnee.

"You'll come back to Wingate with us," she was saying. "We'll take care of you there. Father must know what you did."

Looking up into her tear-shining eyes, he could see she was saying much more. He remembered his poignant need, back at *Yeitso's* Bones, to tell her that he was white, that he could go with her as a man of her own people and not be afraid to tell her he loved her. Now, somehow, that need was not so poignant. His mind was turning over other things. He was remembering how he had killed Yeats, with the ancient Indian weapon of bow and arrow; how he had forced the truth from Clay; how he had crawled across the open ground here without being seen, when Sherwin, a white man, was sighted immediately. All those things were Indian, not white.

It revealed to him more than anything how deeply Indian he really was. Could he change from that, after twenty years? Did he even want to change? It made him think of Pepper. Aye, the man was symbolical of what happened to an Indian who tried to become white.

Tahnee stared up at Iris, realizing that the gulf still lay between them. In essence, even though his parents had been white, his true origins did not lie there. They were here at Kintyel, with the sand painting and the six sacred birds and *Hatali* Anaji. He stood up painfully, and spoke.

49

"No. I cannot come with you." He saw a great hurt darken her face. Then a beginning of comprehension crept through. Tears shone in her eyes. Tahnee turned to Sherwin. "Take good care of her. You are more worthy than I."

Sherwin silently held out his hand. Tahnee clasped it. Then he walked back through the ruins to his horse. It was dark in the valley but the sun still touched the hilltops with its last red rays. It silhouetted him as he rode over the ridge, turning back to give them one last look, and then riding on, a proud and savage figure making a night ride to return to his people.

Six-Gun Snare

Les Savage, Jr.'s original title for this story was "Six-Gun Snare." It was sold to *Star Western*, and the author was paid $225 on March 11, 1944. It was published in the August, 1944 issue under the title "Water Rights — Bought in Hell!" For its appearance here, the author's title and text have been restored.

CHAPTER
ONE

Dirk Hood stood on the curb where the Caldwell-San Antone stage had deposited him, for a moment unaware of the strange hush that had settled over Caprock. It had been four years since he'd stood here on Second Street, with the white alkali dust sifting up from beneath his boots and filling his mouth with that familiar gritty taste — as acrid and bitter as all the hate and fighting and killing that had swept this town from its beginnings.

There were young things about Dirk Hood, standing there, and old things. The skin across the high plane of his cheek was pale from some long confinement, and smooth. But his mouth was drawn too thinly for youth, and his eyes held a cautious, almost secretive look. His black hair was beginning to grow long again beneath an ancient flat-topped Stetson. He had a good breadth to his shoulders beneath the faded gray coat, and his legs fitted the brass-riveted Levi's with a slight horse-collar bow.

He carried a denim war sack under one arm, filled with his few belongings. It was the only thing Caprock had seen him take with him four years ago; it was the only thing Caprock would see him bring back. The other things he had taken away and had brought back were deeply inside him, and he meant to keep them there.

Mickey Walker's spotted hound trotted across the intersection of Second and Mesa, half a block east of Dirk, disappearing into Kruger's Barns on the northwest corner. The movement drew Dirk's attention to the strange quietude lying over the town. He felt a sudden catch at his throat that wasn't the dust. He knew that stillness. There was something special about it.

The same silence had gripped Caprock four years ago, when Dirk had stood across the street by Kruger's big frame barns, waiting for Hugh Glendenning to step out of the covered stairway that led down from the second story of the red brick bank on this side. Waiting with a gun, because that was how Hugh Glendenning had told him to come.

The snort of a horse turned Dirk's head. They had escaped his notice, standing at the corner of Hammer's bank, so they could see all four ways from the intersection. There were three men, sitting horses with the Keyhole brand showing dimly on dusty rumps, holding two empty horses. Dirk Hood squinted his eyes to recognize Lige Glendenning.

Then the covered stairway leading down the south wall of the bank from the Land Office above trembled to the hard-heeled descent of two men. They stepped onto the sidewalk one after the other, swept Second with a swift glance, and moved toward the horses.

54

The one leading was Lige's father, Orson Glendenning. He owned the Keyhole outfit. Hugh Glendenning had been his only brother. He was a tall man, Orson, with the long square jaw of one who might be hard to put off his single-track once he got going on it. His black Mormon set squarely on iron-gray hair that was cropped short on his bony skull. The six-gun that drew its bulge beneath his town coat held its own ominous significance; he was known as a man who never wore a gun unless he meant to use it.

He spoke to his son before he reached the corner and, in the silence, the words carried plainly to Dirk. "I told you Hammer wouldn't give us the loan, Lige. He's Kruger's man now, just like all the rest."

Then Orson must have seen how intently Lige was looking past him down Second. He stopped speaking, and turned to follow his son's gaze down beyond the bank to where Dirk Hood stood in front of the stage office. Dirk saw the slow stiffening of his gaunt body. Then Orson Glendenning turned around and began to come back toward Dirk; the Keyhole hand who had accompanied him followed. Lige said something to the pair of mounted men, climbed off his horse, and came after his father. Their boots made a hollow *rattle* on the plank walk. It was the only sound.

Dirk shifted his war sack beneath his arm. He knew what was coming. Part of it was that the Glendennings led the South Fork faction, and that four years ago Dirk Hood had ridden for the North Fork bunch, and that it had always been this way between the two factions when they met in Caprock. Most of it was that Hugh

55

Glendenning had been Orson's brother, and Lige's uncle.

Orson Glendenning stopped in front of Dirk, leaning forward tensely when he spoke, disbelief in his voice. "Dirk Hood. I thought you were sent up for life."

Dirk didn't answer. There was nothing for him to say. Orson Glendenning spoke again, anger sweeping away the surprised sound in his voice. "You were paroled," he stated. "Kruger finally swung it."

Dirk nodded, still not speaking, feeling the clammy sweat forming beneath his armpits. He could see thin hate twisting into Lige's face.

"And you can come back here," said Lige venomously. "You can come back here and stand in the very street you stood in to murder my uncle."

Dirk felt his own anger rising. "Lige . . ."

"He was your friend," said Lige, taking a vicious step forward. "Hugh was the only decent man you ever called your friend in your life, Dirk Hood, and you murdered him."

"Shut up!" Dirk's voice seemed to explode from him. "I didn't come back to talk about it. What do you suppose I've been thinking about the last four years? Talking like that doesn't help now. I know what I did."

Lige moved in till his face wasn't a foot from Dirk's. "I told you never to let me see you in Caprock again, Hood."

Orson grabbed at his son's arm. "Wait a minute, Lige. How do you know Kruger didn't put Hood out here for just this purpose?"

56

Lige shook his father's hand off and reached out to grab Dirk by the lapels, yanking him off balance. "Maybe he did. I hope so. Things might as well finish here and now."

"Take your hands off me," said Dirk Hood.

"You're leaving, Hood!" said Lige Glendenning in a gusty voice. "You turn around and march out of Caprock and don't ever come back, or, by God, I'll give you the worst pistol-whipping Texas ever watched."

He gasped suddenly. Dirk's hand was closed on his wrist, tearing his fingers from the coat lapel. With a harsh curse, Lige jerked backward and tried to yank his arm free. Dirk flung Lige's wrist down and away from him.

"Lige!" yelled Orson, jumping at them.

Lige's face twisted savagely as he whipped one of his Colts out and above his head, lunging back at Dirk. Hood bent forward suddenly, swinging his war sack from beneath his arm and jamming it upward. Lige was plunging in and couldn't stop the downswinging gun from slamming into the denim sack where Dirk held it above his head.

Dirk felt the war sack *thud* against his shoulder from the force of the blow. He let go of it and hit Lige in the stomach. Then Orson's weight crashed in from one side and the Keyhole hand struck him from the other.

In a moment Dirk was the center of the struggling mass. His head rocked as Lige struck again with his gun. He gasped as the Keyhole rider came in with a knee lifted into his belly. Then Dirk lurched on forward into Lige and caught him in the stomach, knocking him off the curb. Whirling, Dirk grabbed Orson about his spare middle and jerked him around into the cowhand. He lowered his shoulder against Orson and shoved him and the rider off the curb and into Lige who was just getting up, and they all went down in a heap.

Dirk was on his feet like a cat, kicking free of Lige's clawing hand, turning sharply from one man to the other, panting, bent forward a little with his arms out. Orson jumped backward and shoved his coat away from his gun. Lige drew his second Colt and lifted it without trying to rise. A mounted Keyhole man fought his rearing horse around to aim his Winchester at Dirk.

"That'll do, damn you, that'll do!"

Dirk saw Lige's Colt stop coming up, saw Orson halt with his coat held back from a weapon half drawn. Dirk turned toward the intersection, from where the booming voice had come. Sheriff Mickey Walker shook the earth as he descended from the high curb to the rutted street and walked down to them. The sheriff had a big Peacemaker in his horny fist. His eyes blazed like a ringy bull's from the apoplectic red of his face, and every time he took a step his snow-white goatee bobbed in rhythm to the angry quiver of his paunch. He reached the group and planted his size-twelve Hyers in the ground like post oaks. He shoved his ten-gallon back on a mane of white hair.

"Lige Glendenning," he thundered, "you and your whole clan get on those horses and race back to the Keyhole, or I'll throw you in the *calabozo* for disturbing the peace. Dirk Hood's here on parole and I'm responsible for his conduct. No herring-gutted South Fork man's going to cause any trouble with him!"

Lige picked up the gun he had dropped and stood there a moment, trembling with rage. Breathing heavily, Orson walked over to him. The older man drew his son toward the horses. Lige mounted his dish-faced mare; he swung it so he faced Dirk from the saddle.

"All right," he said. "Don't think this'll help, Hood. Don't think you're staying here . . . you or Kruger or Kruger's fat tin badge. You're all going! Just remember that, Hood."

Sheriff Mickey Walker stood there in the dusty street, watching the five horsemen turn the corner at Mesa and lift a cloud of dust southward toward the Keyhole. Finally the lawman turned to Dirk. "Tarnation, son," he said. "How do you expect to stay out of jail on good behavior when the first thing you do back in town is start a ruckus?"

"I didn't want it that way, Mick," said Dirk heavily. "But it was bound to happen. How did you swing the parole? I thought Orson was fighting it?"

"Things have changed in Caprock, Dirk," said Walker, putting his gun away. "When you rode for Jess Kruger, he was the underdog, and Glendenning sat the saddle here. But the cinch has busted under Orson. The South Fork's drying up."

Dirk had bent to pick up his war sack. He straightened, a strange tight look on his face. South Fork drying up? That was incomprehensible. Twenty miles west of the town site, the Río Cabezon forked into two branches, the South Fork running below

59

Caprock, the North Fork turning above. Dirk Hood's father had pioneered here with Hugh Glendenning, Orson's brother. From their original quarter sections, both men had spread out, until John Hood's Keyhole outfit and Glendenning's H-Bar-H controlled all the water of the South Fork.

Whatever newcomers arrived after that had to be satisfied with the grass and water of the North Fork, which was already showing signs of drying up. One of these newcomers had been Jess Kruger. Kruger's refusal to submit to the stronger South Fork group had started a feud that grew until Caprock was known from Oklahoma to Mexico as a town where a man would find lead pushing his breakfast out backward if he so much as struck a match on the wrong side of Second Street. And throughout that long bitter war, it had always been Jess Kruger fighting from the bottom. Now . . .

Walker saw the look in Dirk's eyes, and he nodded. "With the South Fork drying up, Orson and his bunch don't swing any more rope than Jess Kruger. Just as many of their cattle died this summer as Jess's did. Just as many of them have first and second mortgages on their spreads. You saw how Orson went out. It's Kruger's town now. He ain't the underdog any more. I think that's partly why you rode for him. You was always a kind to pull for the underdog."

"Partly," said Dirk. "Mostly because I thought I hated Hugh Glendenning more than any man on earth. He and Dad built this country together, Mick. For sixteen years I thought Hugh was the best friend Dad

60

and I had. How could he turn on me that way when Dad died, Mick?"

The sheriff dropped his hand on Dirk's shoulder. "You've got to remember none of your friends could help you that time, Dirk. Hugh was in the same fix as everybody else, Dirk. He didn't have a dime left after that winter."

Dirk shook his head. "I believed Hugh at first, when I went to him for help and he told me he couldn't do anything. Then Orson Glendenning came from Chicago and bought the Keyhole at bank sale. Not six months after I'd lost it because Hugh said he couldn't help me. What else could it look like?"

"You didn't let it look like anything else," said Mick, not meeting his eyes. "I can't say as I blame you. On the surface it did look like he sold you out. There was other folks thought the same thing for a long time afterward. I guess it made you pretty mad. Did you think you'd get even with Hugh, signing up with Kruger that way?"

Dirk drew a heavy breath. "I don't know, Mick. I was all mixed up. Maybe Uncle El was right. He tried to make me stay out of the feud. He said it took a stronger man to stay in the middle than it took to take sides. He said I'd end up regretting what I did, whichever side I rode for. I'm telling him that now, Mick. I'm telling him that he was right."

Dirk felt the sheriff's hand tighten on his shoulder. "Kid," said Walker, "your Uncle El . . . your uncle's dead."

Dirk stood there a long moment, a heavy constriction in his chest. Abstractedly he was aware that the town had come to life again. A group of Jess Kruger's Long Shank riders had moved out of the hardware store on the northeast corner of Second and Mesa, were standing on the sidewalk beneath the overhang, holding Winchesters. A man crossed from Kruger's Barns to the bank, looking southward down Mesa after the Keyhole bunch. The shock was gone now, and Dirk felt the first grief.

"When did he die?" he asked almost inaudibly.

"Just after you were sent up," said Mick. "Almost four years ago. We found him in his barn with his head knocked in . . ." He cut off as Dirk's pale face jerked up; there was a sharp, twisted look to the boy's mouth. Mick nodded. "We don't know who did it. They used one of his own hammers."

"But why?" Dirk almost whispered. "Why? An old man like that, without an enemy in the world . . . My uncle's things," Dirk added suddenly. "Where are they?"

Mick opened his mouth a little. "His what?"

"His things," repeated Dirk harshly. "His tools, his forge. I told you how it was going to be. I came back to tell Uncle El he'd been right, and to live in this town the way he wanted me to. I didn't come back to shoot anybody."

Mick's eyes widened beneath shaggy white brows. "Listen, kid, we all know how you felt about Hugh Glendenning. We don't blame you for what happened, even for sending him that note . . ."

"I didn't send any note," said Dirk hotly. "I got one from him, saying to meet him at Second and Mesa, two o'clock that day, with my gun out."

"OK, OK," said Mickey Walker, tightening the hand on his shoulder. "It doesn't matter. But you can't let it affect you this way, kid. None of us blame you for what happened. He sent you a note saying to meet him that way. What else could you do when you saw him step out of Slagel's stairway and saw his hand move. If your shot hadn't killed Hugh, Seeco Smith's would have, or some other Long Shanker's. You know how the fireworks started the minute you pulled your gun."

"He was unarmed, Mick," said Dirk hoarsely. "He was just raising his hand and I thought he was drawing, and I murdered him."

"You didn't know that," said Mick.

Dirk's face was white and set. "Did you ever stay awake most of the night, night after night, for four years, knowing you'd killed a man who'd been your best friend as long as you'd lived? Do you think I'd pack a gun for Jess Kruger again?"

"But Jess sprung you," said the sheriff tightly. "You can't buck him now. You know what'll happen if you try it. He owns Caprock, and, if you don't, he'll get rid of you just as fast as he would a South Forker."

"Or my uncle?" said Dirk, and felt Mick's hand slide from his arm, saw Mick's face turn suddenly pale. "Where are my uncle's things, Mick?"

CHAPTER
TWO

Clyde Slagel's office was on the second story of
Hammer's red-brick bank. It was a comfortable,
furnished room, its sagging leather armchairs and huge
littered desk reflecting Slagel's easy-going disposition.
Slagel himself sat with his swivel chair tilted back, feet
propped up on the desk. He wore a blue Prince Albert
and pin-striped trousers. His hair was graying at the
temples, giving him a mildly distinguished look. He was
smiling beneath a small, clipped mustache.

"Sheriff Walker was right, Dirk," he said pleasantly.
"I handled El Hood's estate. There was no kin to do it,
with your father dead, and you . . . ah . . . upstate. El
had some debts and his barn and lot went for them.
There was some old equipment, along with his personal
effects, that I couldn't get rid of. You'll find them stored
in the rear end of Kruger's Barns."

From where he stood, Dirk could read the sign on
the glass of the window:

Clyde Slagel
United States Land Office.

Beyond that, across Second, was the two-story, paint-peeled side wall of Kruger's Barns. Clyde Slagel's pet black crow hopped across the desk, fluttering through the mess of papers.

"There's something more, Mister Slagel," said Dirk. "About Uncle El."

Clyde Slagel's smile faded a little. "I suppose you want my ideas?"

"Not unless you want to give them," said Dirk stiffly.

Slagel shrugged. "I have none, Dirk. He was found dead some weeks after you were sent up. That's all I know."

Dirk's face hardened. "I understand how it is. You and my uncle were about the only men in town who didn't belong to one side or the other."

Slagel took some bread crumbs from a drawer and began to feed the crow. "And now I'm the only one left, is that what you meant? I'm not afraid of Jess Kruger, Dirk. If I had any ideas, you'd be first to hear them. But I haven't. There wasn't any reason to kill your uncle. You find me a reason and maybe I'll find some ideas. Isn't that right, Edgar?"

"Nevermore," rasped the crow.

Slagel laughed softly again, then turned to his son who lounged in one of the leather chairs. "Victor, you take Dirk over and unlock that storeroom of Kruger's."

Victor Slagel had none of his father's refinement. He was a big, top-heavy man in his middle twenties, with heavy black hair that fell, unbrushed, over a low forehead. He wore a smith's apron over the knotty bulge of his shoulders. The hand he jerked at Dirk was callused and grimed from the forge.

"You aren't going to let him . . . ?" he began.

"Victor," said Clyde Slagel, feeding his crow another crumb, "we owe Dirk what help we can give him. If he's going to stay out of the fight like his Uncle El did, it makes him one of us. Just because you work at Kruger's forge doesn't mean you're Kruger's man. I thought we had that out a time back. If you don't like real estate, that's all right with me. But don't you get to thinking like a Kruger man. A town should be a place where you can live as you want and think as you want and do as you want. Don't you agree, Edgar?"

"Nevermore," croaked the crow.

"Thanks, Mister Slagel," said Dirk. "How about a place to set up in? I got ten dollars when they released me. It'd do for a first month's rent till I got started."

Slagel pursed his lips. "Kruger owns more of Caprock than he used to, Dirk. Whatever I hold is rented."

"Who holds that vacant lot?"

Victor's mouth sagged. "Across from Kruger's?"

Clyde Slagel began to laugh, then he got up. "Yes, Victor, across from Kruger's. What other kind of boy did you think Dirk Hood was? The vacant lot across from Kruger's. I hold it, Dirk. And if you want to set up there, you go right ahead."

His soft laugh followed them out the door and down the stairs, and Dirk didn't know whether he liked it or not.

Sullenly Victor went with Dirk across the street and into Kruger's. Dirk followed him down the lane between the stalls to where several Long Shank riders lounged around the forges at the rear of the big frame barns. Seeco Smith sat on an unused anvil. When Dirk had begun to ride for Kruger, it had been Seeco who taught the boy gun savvy. And when the time came for the meeting between Dirk Hood and Hugh Glendenning, Seeco's teaching had turned Dirk's draw into an instinctive reaction that he didn't even have to think about — until it was too late to think.

Seeco's flannel shirt hung loosely on a slat-limbed torso, tucked into the tight waistband of rawhide *chivarras* that served him for pants. There was nothing fancy about the way he wore his wooden-handled Remington; the only thing that marked his talent was the myriad of faint scars across the top part of his worn holster, which might have come from the constant scrape of fingernails over the leather.

"Hello, Dirk," he said without smiling. "I hear you're going to watch the roundup from the fence."

The towering blacksmith had stopped working his bellows. A silence had settled over the barns. The other Kruger men were watching Dirk intently. From up front a horse snorted.

The hand Seeco Smith rubbed across his sandy three-day growth of whiskers did not show any rope burns. "It hits men that way sometimes. Maybe you remember I told you that. Shoot their first man and they lose their guts. I wouldn't have wasted my time on you if I'd've thought you were that kind."

Dirk took a small, jerky step toward him. Seeco didn't move. His pale blue eyes were old and wise behind their wind-wrinkled lids. Dirk took a heavy breath, then he turned to Victor, jerking his head. Victor went on past the forge, and Dirk followed. Behind him he heard the hollow *puffing* sound of the bellows start up again. He could feel the nails of his closed fingers digging into the flesh of his palms.

El Hood's old anvil stood beside his pile of rusting tools in the storeroom at the very rear. Dirk picked up a hoof chisel, toed at some corroded nail nippers. Beneath them lay a strange three-pronged object in the form of a Y, with a torn buckskin sack on the end of one prong. The leather of the sack looked slick and gummy, as if it had been pitched to make it waterproof.

"That isn't Uncle El's," said Dirk.

"That's Clyde's," said Victor, picking it up swiftly. "Since the South Fork started drying up, Orson Glendenning's been hunting for a dome of water underground. Figures it must be somewhere around here because the Rio Cabezon rises from underground. Clyde's been using this water witch to help him locate it."

"Found any water?"

"No," said Victor almost defensively, "but I've seen it work. You hold the two forks in your hand with the sack full of water hanging toward the ground. They use it the same way to find a dome of oil, or minerals . . . except they fill the sack with oil, or put in a silver dollar or gold piece on the bottom prong. When you get directly over the water or oil, the witch begins shaking like a spooked horse. I've seen it happen."

"Not around here, though," muttered Dirk, squatting to sort through the tools. "Where's the tin box?"

Victor Slagel seemed to hesitate. "What tin box?"

Dirk stood up, turning to him. "Uncle El had a tin box of personals. Locked. He told me some of Dad's stuff was in it. Said Dad had left me something they couldn't take away with all the mortgages in Texas. Said I'd get it when I was of age."

Victor was even more sullen. "We didn't find no tin box."

Dirk moved toward him. "Don't lie to me, Victor."

"Listen," said Victor, "call me a liar again and you won't even get this much. Now take your junk and get out."

For a moment they stood face to face. Close up, Dirk saw how big a man Victor really was. He stood a head above Dirk, and his work at the forge had filled out his shoulders and chest until their tremendous bulk appeared almost grotesque, even above his broad hips and solid legs. Dirk felt his lips draw back against his teeth; the anger in him settled to a slow dull burn.

He spoke with difficulty. "I'll need a wagon for the forge."

Victor nodded to a buckboard with a horse already in its hitch up ahead of them. "Clyde's rig. I've been shoeing his dun."

Jess Kruger had several hoists for loading his feed and lifting his sick horses — heavy chains suspended from runners that worked in steel tracks along the rafters. Dirk went over to the nearest one and began pulling it across to the forge.

"You're wasting a lot of time," growled Victor. "If you don't get out of here before Kruger comes, you'll have trouble."

He moved deliberately to the large forge. It took a moment for Dirk to realize the man's intention. Slagel bent and put his thick-fingered hands carefully under the two ends of the forge. He set his legs close together; his sweat-stained shirt suddenly drew tautly about the muscle humping up across his shoulders. He lifted the forge.

Dirk realized he had let his jaw sag slightly; he clamped it shut. He had never seen anyone lift a forge single-handed like that, and he had seen plenty of smiths proud of their strength. The buckboard shuddered and settled as Slagel heaved the ponderous mass of iron over its tailgate. He turned, wiping sweat from his low forehead, mouth still twisted sullenly. Dirk put in the smaller anvils and dumped the tools under the seat. He turned and gigged the dun forward past Seeco Smith and the others, toward the door. A man came in from outside, silhouetted by the light at first so that Dirk didn't recognize him.

"Where do you think you're going with that rig?" he asked.

It was Jess Kruger. Dirk stopped the buckboard, squinting his eyes to see the owner of the Long Shank against the light. He was a big black-haired man, Kruger, as solid and beefy as the Polled Angus bulls he ran on his North Fork spread. The ruthlessness of the man was evident in his atavistic beak of a nose, jutting sharply from beneath a brow that was shaped like one of the granite crags in Yellow Horse Cañon. He stood with his black tailcoat hanging over a hand stuffed in his right pants pocket; with his other hand he removed the cold stogie from thin, hard lips.

"Dirk," he said. "Didn't recognize you. I wondered where you disappeared to after that ruckus in the street. Wanted to welcome you back."

"Thanks, Jess," said Dirk. "I heard you were responsible for my parole."

"I told you I'd spring you if I ever got the chance, kid," said Kruger, spitting and putting his cigar back in his mouth. "Glendenning brought pressure to bear whenever I tried it before. But his political pull is gone now, without any water to back him. You saw what happened this morning. It was his last bid. He's sold everything but his saddle for money to sink those wells, and he hasn't found that underground reservoir yet. We expected Orson to blow up when Hammer refused him another loan today. Maybe he would have, too. He came in with his gun. I'm not saying you stopped him, but you sure snubbed his dally enough to interrupt him. Going riding?"

"These are Uncle El's things," said Dirk. "I'm taking them."

Kruger nodded, took out his cigar, and studied it a moment. "Too bad about your uncle, Dirk. Nobody could figure who'd do a low-down thing like that. We'll try and make it up to you. There's a bunk waiting for you in my rooming house over the hardware, and any horse in my string is yours. I'm glad you're back. Orson Glendenning is through, and he knows it, but he isn't going out without a fight. It just depends on whose fork goes bone-dry first. Either way, you'll see a war that'll make the past ten years' fighting look like a sick dogie. I'll need a man who can handle his guns like you . . ."

He broke off suddenly, still holding his stogie, and looked up at Dirk with a strange expression. Seeco Smith had drifted up from the rear; he was watching Kruger intently. Dirk sensed the shift of other Long Shank riders behind him. He tightened his reins a little.

"Where did you say you were going with El's stuff?" asked Kruger.

Seeco Smith stood beside the wagon now. He held his right fist up against his chest. It was a sign men who know Seeco Smith could read well enough. Dirk knew Seeco Smith.

"I tried to explain it to Mick this morning, Jess," Dirk said, "but he didn't understand. I know you won't. Nobody can understand until they've been through it themselves. I won't try to tell you why. I just didn't come back to ride for you, that's all. I'm setting up for myself."

Kruger didn't seem surprised. He looked at his cigar a long time. The two Long Shank cowpunchers had come up to stand beside Seeco Smith now. Victor Slagel had come around the tailgate with the other blacksmith. Kruger put his cigar back into his thin lips and clamped them shut.

"Yeah," he said finally. "Yeah. Mick told me about that a few minutes ago. Orson, then?"

"No," said Dirk, "I didn't come back to ride for him, either."

"Your uncle tried that, kid," said Kruger. "It can't be done. There are only two sides in Caprock. A man's either with me or with Orson Glendenning. I sprung you Dirk . . ."

"You sprung me all right," said Dirk, "to use me. Maybe you used me in the first place to get rid of Hugh. I came back thinking I owed you something, Jess. I'm beginning to wonder."

Kruger flushed. He took his hand from his pocket, seeming to control himself with an effort. "If you want to be a smith, you can have a job at my forge."

Dirk shook his head. "What's the difference, riding your horse or working your bellows? I'd be your man."

The anger Kruger had been holding suddenly trembled through him. He took his cigar out, stabbing it at Dirk.

"Then get off that wagon. You aren't taking anything out of my barns."

"They're my things, and this is Slagel's wagon," said Dirk, blood beginning to pound in him.

Seeco had a strange, taut look to his narrow face; the fist held against his chest was white at the knuckles. Kruger grabbed the dun's bridle, half shouting.

"Dirk, if you don't get off that rig, we'll take you off!"

Dirk was surprised at how quiet his voice sounded. "Jess, don't do that, don't try to stop me."

"Take him off!" Kruger yelled hoarsely. "Drag him off there!"

Dirk was already bending sideways as the men surged forward. In a blur, he saw Seeco's white fist flash down toward that Remington as he leaped toward the wagon — saw the twisted faces of the Long Shank riders behind Seeco — felt the buck-board shudder and tilt as the blacksmith swung over its side farther back.

Then Dirk was standing erect suddenly, and the sun coming in through the big double doors glinted across the metal of one of El Hood's tools.

"You ever been hit in the head by a hoof hammer?" he yelled.

Seeco hadn't quite freed his gun. The surprise twisting his face was almost ludicrous. Instinctively he recoiled, dropping his hand from the springs of the wagon seat and taking a step back into the Long Shank cowpunchers, knocking them away. For that moment, Dirk's lean tense young figure, standing rigidly above them with that hammer, held the men.

The sudden pound of boots across Mesa Street from outside broke the spell.

"It's Doc Alcott!" a young man shouted from out there. "His mare's run away with him again. She's coming down Second. She'll take the turn sure. He'll be killed this time."

From the doorway, Dirk could see the black buggy clattering suddenly into view down Second Street. Dr. Alcott was thrown back from the seat, with his feet kicking air helplessly, and the reins were dropped into the doubletree. A rider was lashing his cow pony into the mare and leaning out to grab the harness. But Doc Alcott's house was up at First and Mesa, and at

74

the corner of Second the mare took its habitual turn. The man on the cow pony was slammed away from the mare's flank. The careening buggy struck him and knocked his horse aside, and he jumped free as the cow pony stumbled and went down.

"The buggy'll drag her!" shouted Victor Slagel. "She'll never make that full turn! She'll smash right in on us!"

The men around Dirk scattered back into the barn, yelling. Dirk dropped the hoof hammer. He jumped out of the buckboard and ran into the street. The mare was pounding around Kruger's Hardware on the opposite corner, buggy tilting crazily on one rear wheel. But already the drag was evident. The animal would never make a complete turn.

Dirk cut down the front wall of the barns to the corner across from the hardware. By the time he reached the end of the wall, the mare was fully into Mesa, heading diagonally across toward the barns, unable to turn farther with the buggy crashing around behind on one wheel and pulling on it. Dirk was south of the line the horse would take when he turned away from the barns. He quartered in on the animal, allowing her to come on his flank, flinging himself toward her from the side. For one blind moment he felt the slap of gritty dust in his face and the sound of thundering hoofs shaking the ground beneath him and the terrific impact of the brute's sweaty shoulder against his chest. Then his hand clutched the mane, and his other arm hooked around the neck. He jumped into the air with his grip acting as a lever upon which the mare's momentum, added to his own, swung him up and over onto her.

With his left foot on one tree and his right leg kicking over the horse, he grabbed blindly for the off rein. He was dimly aware of the big-frame barns looming up ahead, rushing toward him. He found the rein, and the horse's head jerked to his sudden pull. The buggy shuddered behind them, tilting crazily over onto its left wheel again as the horse spun under Dirk's desperate rein. The boy fought the animal, kept pulling savagely on the ribbon. The barns were directly ahead and he got a blurred impression of the towering, paint-peeled walls and the buck-board standing in the gloom of the doorway and the shouts of the men farther back inside. Slagel's dun whinnied and reared as the mare came charging at it.

Gasping, Dirk yanked for the last savage time on the off rein. The horse turned on farther up Mesa, dragging the buggy and all, and the barns were suddenly on their flank instead of ahead. Dirk's left leg was almost torn off as the horse followed the building wall down, ripping a board out with the end of the left tree.

The mare's rump slammed against the wall as Dirk pulled it out and away. The buggy crashed against the building behind them, and the collision knocked it upright again. The mare jumped the corner wildly, and the buggy crashed across the planks behind them, wheels *popping* and *screeching*.

Dirk lay limply on the mare, feet hooked into the trees. He heard the buggy dragging behind them and knew it had dished a wheel going over the sidewalk.

The quivering animal hauled the wrecked outfit clear across the street, and wouldn't be stopped till she reached the white picket fence surrounding Alcott's big house up near First.

There was already a crowd around the horse when Dirk slid off. The buggy's whole left side was a mess of ripped black leather and broken hoops. The left wheel had collapsed and some men were helping Alcott out of the buggy where it had dragged to a stop. Doc Alcott's housekeeper, a big motherly lady with her gray hair in a bun, wouldn't allow anybody inside but the doctor and Dirk Hood. She plumped Alcott down on the living-room couch and fussed around.

"Woman," said the doctor peevishly, "I'm all right. Just shaken up a bit. You go and put something on the stove."

She stood back from him, hands on her ample hips. "Put what on the stove?"

Alcott was a rotund little man, brows forming a fuzzy line above round blue eyes set in a pink face. He wore an archaic fustian with a huge silver watch chain across his white waistcoat. He waved his hand vaguely.

"Coffee, tea, anything. I don't care. Just put it on the stove."

"I declare," she said, turning to Dirk, "this is a fine homecoming for you. I certainly ain't going to waste my time making coffee. What you need is some horse liniment and hot water, both of you."

She flounced off through the sliding doors leading to the dining room, muttering to herself.

Doc Alcott straightened with a heavy breath. "That woman," he chuckled, shaking his head. Then his smile faded and he looked up. "So you came back, Dirk Hood?"

Dirk nodded, rubbing a bruised elbow, feeling as if a herd of whitefaces had run over him all night. Alcott rose suddenly, grunting with the effort. He went to the mantle and stood there a long time, faced away from Dirk. Through Mrs. Fowler's starched curtains on the big front window, Dirk could see some Long Shank riders trying to unhitch the excited mare from the wrecked tree.

"You saved my life, boy, but I guess you know that."

Alcott's voice startled Dirk. He turned. "I just . . ."

"You saved my life," said the doctor almost angrily, waving a pink hand at the couch. "Sit down, Dirk. I've got something I want to tell you. It's preyed on me four years now. Millie's dead. She was a good wife, and she died two years ago."

Dirk's eyes darkened in sympathy. "I'm sorry . . ."

Alcott nodded. "It won't be long for me now, boy. Things have changed in four years. Millie's gone. I'm on my way. And you saved my life. I don't know why you just didn't let me crash right into Kruger's Barns and break my worthless old cranium wide open."

"Don't talk crazy, Doc."

"I'm not talking crazy," said Alcott, brushing dust from his coat absently. "I'm talking straight for the first time in four years. I had Millie before, Dirk. You've got to understand that. I was Jess Kruger's man and I knew what would happen if I said the wrong thing. Just like your uncle . . . ."

Dirk stood suddenly. "You think Kruger . . . ?"

Alcott drew a heavy breath. "I don't know. You can't be neutral in this town. I don't know why El Hood was killed or by whom. I just know I would have gotten the same thing if I'd talked wrong. More than that, I was afraid for Millie. You know Kruger. You've got to understand."

Dirk grabbed his arm. "What are you trying to tell me?"

"As the doctor attending when you had the run-in with Hugh Glendenning," said Alcott, "I was called on to testify at the trial. I said that death had come instantly from the only bullet that struck him."

"I never blamed you," said Dirk. "It was a simple statement of facts."

"Not all the facts," said Alcott, breath suddenly coming faster. "I testified that the bullet struck his head. But there was more than that. I didn't tell the jury that the bullet had entered the top part of Hugh Glendenning's frontalis and passed through his brain to lodge in the axis vertebra. If it had gone out, I couldn't have gotten away with it. But there was no point of exit and a layman couldn't tell the direction of that slug's passage. I could. Frontalis to axis, Dirk . . . ." He stopped, turning toward the two men who had come in through the front door. Jess Kruger and Clyde Slagel.

"Heard about the excitement, Doc," said Clyde Slagel, smiling. "Thought I'd drop in and see how you were. What's that about a frontalis?"

CHAPTER
THREE

The leather had rotted off El Hood's old bellows, and Dirk set about sewing new hide onto the frame that next morning, hunkered down in the shade of the willows at the back end of Slagel's lot between Alcott's white house and Kruger's Hardware. Jess Kruger had still been at the doctor's with Slagel when Dirk had left, and most of the Long Shank riders were still trying to get the horse extricated from the smashed tree without any more damage. Only Seeco Smith and Victor Slagel were in the doorway of the barns when Dirk went back to get the buckboard with his forge and tools.

He was finishing the rawhide stitching on his bellows when a sudden shriek jerked his head up. Jess Kruger had offices on the second story of his barns across Mesa. Dirk saw that one of the windows had made that sound, being shoved up. Kruger stood there, looking southward down Mesa, cigar clamped in his mouth. Mick Walker came out of the courthouse up at First and Mesa, his boots making a resounding *clatter* on the plank sidewalk. In front of the Jaykay Saloon he stopped suddenly, looking, open-mouthed, down the street. In the sudden silence, his voice carried clearly to Dirk.

"Tarnation," he said. "Terry Glendenning!"

Dirk moved to the front end of the lot where he could see south down Mesa Street. Orson Glendenning's daughter, Terry, was coming up from the south. She was trotting her pinto up the center of the street, looking neither to right nor left. And she was coming alone. The girl sat straight in the saddle, a slim figure in a flannel shirt and cream-colored cowhide vest, her hat shoved off her head and bobbing against her back, held there by the tie-thongs around her neck. She reached the vacant lot and turned in. Once, before Orson had bought the Keyhole, there had been things between Dirk and this girl that were brought back to him now, by the way the sunlight played through her wind-blown hair, turning the deep chestnut color to flickering gold.

"Terry," he said. "Are you crazy, coming into town alone?"

She swung down. "You're here, aren't you? Alone. I understand you're going to take up your uncle's trade. My pinto needs shoes, Dirk."

He didn't understand it for a moment; he held out his hand. "But you ... you're a Glendenning ... you ..."

"I should hate you, like Lige and Dad?" she supplied. "You know I never could, Dirk. Maybe for the first few days after it happened. Not any longer. And there were so many odd things about it. Those notes. It isn't logical that two men, neither of them knowing what the other was doing, should each write the other a note naming an identical place and time for a meeting like that."

"How many times do you think I tried to tell them that at the trial?" he said, and glanced at Kruger's Barns, with the open window of the office above.

She caught the glance. "Dirk, you don't think somebody . . . ?"

"If Hugh Glendenning got a note," said Dirk, "somebody else besides me sent it. I don't know who or why. I've tried to figure it out, but nothing adds up. Nobody stood to gain anything by getting Hugh out of the way. It wouldn't weaken the South Fork bunch any. Your dad just took the lead with Hugh gone. But it isn't that troubling me most, Terry . . ."

He bent to get the pinto's reins. When he straightened, his glance met the girl's. He realized suddenly that she understood what he had gone through the past four years, knowing he had killed a man who'd been as close a friend as Hugh. It was in her eyes. Maybe he couldn't explain it to Mick, or the others, but he didn't have to explain it to Terry.

He hitched the horse to the tree, then lifted a hoof. "You should know better than to let a horse go this long without refitting, Terry. Look at those side bones."

"All our horses are that way, Dirk," she said. "Your Uncle El did all our refitting. When he died, Kruger's Barns was the only place left. You know what a chance we had there. Dad wouldn't even ask Kruger. We tried to do our own refitting. It might have worked on grassland, but not in the Caprock country. The horses began throwing those homemade shoes right away. We need an experienced farrier, Dirk. Another week or so and we won't have any horses to ride. They're all crippled up like this."

Dirk bent to cut the heads of the nails from the old shoe with the clinch cutters. He said: "Uncle El had some screw-caulked shoes in his kit. They're used, but they're still better than these you've got."

"Dirk," she said huskily, "if we don't get our whole string refitted, we're through. It won't matter whether we have water or not. Without horses, we're through. I promise Lige won't cause any trouble."

He nodded, not meeting her eyes. "I have sent to San Antone for some new shoes. The day they arrive on the stage, I'll be out at your spread."

"Dirk," she whispered in a low voice.

He turned to set up the bellows, smiling faintly. It had been a long time since he'd heard his name said like that. The puff of hot air and the ring of steel on the anvil were welcome, and he settled into shaping the old metal with sweat running down his face. She came around the horse and stood nearby, studying Dirk.

"We tried to explain to you at the time," she said finally, "but you were blind mad and you wouldn't see it. Uncle Hugh never sold you out. You must realize that now. When you went to him for help, he was on the verge of bankruptcy. He had written that to us. That's why we came out. Dad helped him back on his feet and, by the time we decided to settle here, your Keyhole had been in Hammer's hands almost six months. It was next to the H-Bar-H, and being held at sale price by the bank. It was only natural for Dad to take advantage of that."

He nodded. "Four years cools a man down, Terry. Maybe I would have seen it that way sooner if I hadn't started riding for Kruger. Being with the North Forkers that way just naturally kept me all whipped up inside against Hugh and his gang. Let's not talk about any of it any more. I'm tired. I want to forget it. I hear you went to school while I was away."

She nodded. "I wasn't able to finish. The South Fork began to go and Dad had to pull in his horns."

"Nursing?" he said. "Isn't that what Mick told me? Would you know what a frontalis is?"

"Yes, it was nursing," she said, and tapped her forehead. "A frontalis is this. The front of your head."

"And the axis vertebra?"

She smiled. "That's the base of your neck . . ." She trailed off at the sudden look in his eyes. He slipped his hoof hammer into his belt without knowing it. He was staring at Dr. Alcott's white house, and he didn't see it.

"And something entering the top part of the frontalis," he said in a hollow voice, "and passing through the brain to lodge against the axis vertebra, would be coming . . . ?"

"From somewhere above," said Terry. "Why?"

The girl had left, and it was almost dark when Dirk put a tarp over his forges and went down Mesa toward the stage office. He hadn't answered the girl's question; he didn't know the answer.

Mick Walker's spotted hound cut across from the hardware and disappeared into Kruger's Barns. It drew Dirk's glance to the darkened upper windows where

Jess Kruger had his offices. He shook his head, eyes swinging back to the building ahead of him, on his side of Mesa — the false-fronted two-story building with Kruger's Hardware on the bottom floor and rooms above for whatever of Kruger's riders were in town, and for a few paying roomers.

Across Second Street from the hardware, someone lit a cigarette in front of Acto's Dry Goods Emporium, the glow a red pinpoint in the dusk. Acto's was two-storied, also. Hugh Glendenning had kept offices on its top floor before his death.

The soft *click* of Hammer's clerk locking the bank doors for the night came to Dirk, and he was drawn to look from the dry-goods store to the bank on the southwest corner of the intersection. The *clatter* of the clerk's shoes down the sidewalk on Second diminished past the covered stairway leading up to Clyde Slagel's Land Office above.

There they were, then. Four years, Dirk thought. Four years the thought that he had murdered Hugh Glendenning had galled him like a sore that would never heal, haunting him at night, oppressing him during the day. And now . . .

He realized suddenly that the movement in the barns across Mesa had not been Mick's dog coming back out. He could see the man's form now, cutting across the street toward his side of the intersection ahead. Kruger had three blacksmiths working for him; only one of them possessed the breadth of shoulder this man showed. He reached the middle of Mesa about the time Dirk came to the north side of the hardware. He seemed to be carrying something on his shoulder. Dirk caught the turn of the man's head.

"Dirk?"

"You know it is, Victor," said Dirk.

There was a certain deliberate purpose in Victor Slagel's walk, and Dirk suddenly saw what it was he carried on his shoulder. But Clyde Slagel had said . . . What did it matter what Clyde had said? Victor worked for Kruger; he was Kruger's man.

"I hear you're going to do some work for the Glendennings!" called Victor, still moving diagonally across so he would reach the corner of Mesa and Second about the same time Dirk did.

"That's right," said Dirk.

There was no stopping now. His boots made a steady pound on the walk. His hands slipped down to the twelve-pound hoof hammer he carried in his belt.

"You're making a mistake, kid," said Victor Slagel.

Dirk suddenly turned off the walk and into the street directly toward the man. The change of direction seemed to surprise Slagel; he turned, still walking, and shifted the huge sledge-hammer on his shoulder a little. Dirk was remembering how he had seen the man lift the forge in Kruger's Barns.

"I'm making no mistake," said Dirk, and stepped over a wheel rut. "I'll shoe Glendenning's horses if he asks me. I'll shoe Kruger's horses. I'm a blacksmith. I'm not Kruger's man or Glendenning's man. And I'm not making any mistake."

The long-handled sledge must have weighed thirty pounds. Slagel lowered it from his shoulder without any apparent effort and held it in both hands across his belly as he stopped walking and turned there in the middle of the street to face Dirk. The man was close enough for Dirk to see the sullen twist in the boy's mouth. He stepped across another rut, coming forward steadily.

"You could set up shop in any town from here to Montana," said Slagel. "You could take tomorrow's stage north and set up any place you picked."

"Is that Kruger's offer?" said Dirk. "Tell him I'm staying here."

Slagel's voice sounded strained. "I'm giving you a chance, kid. You're making a mistake."

"I'm making no mistake," said Dirk, and took the last step.

His head was turned up and his eyes were wide open. He heard Slagel's tremendous grunt; he saw the sledge swing up over Slagel's head. The man's body was a blur in front of him, lunging forward.

Dirk's boots made a sudden scraping shuffle and he threw himself to one side, lashing out with the hoof hammer at the same time. The sledge crashed down where he had stood a moment before and struck the ground with a shuddering impact. Victor yelled hoarsely as Dirk's hammer struck his arm.

The big man spun, whipping his sledge up and around with that grunting sound. Dirk struck hard with the hammer again, jumping back. The sledge caught at his shirt and tore it from his pants, going on around, its momentum carrying Slagel with it. Before the man could recover, Dirk leaped in, hacking at him. Slagel

87

screamed. He stopped his hammer with a tremendous effort and jerked it back toward Dirk without raising it. The whole length of the sledge's handle slammed into Dirk, knocking him away. He rolled to the ground, pain paralyzing his right side.

With a savage cry, Slagel leaped at him. Dirk saw the sledge coming down. He was still rolling and he jerked his legs desperately into a jackknife, feeling the ground shudder beneath him as the sledge missed his boot heels by inches and *thudded* into the earth. Dirk rolled on over and dived at Slagel, as the man jerked the sledge up. He caught Slagel across the knees with the hoof hammer.

"God damn," sobbed Victor Slagel, and tried to fight away from the vicious little hammer.

Dirk stumbled on forward and kept beating at the man's legs. Cursing with pain, Slagel swung his sledge from the side. It struck Dirk's left shoulder. Slammed to the ground, Dirk heard his own shout of agony. Crying hoarsely, uncontrollably, he caught hold of the sledge before Slagel could lift it again. He climbed halfway up it, slugging at the man's legs. Slagel tried to jerk away. Grunting, Dirk hacked stubbornly at him with the hoof hammer. Slagel gasped sharply and went to his knees, finally managing to jerk the sledge free. He whipped it around behind him.

Dirk sprawled over Slagel and caught the sledge, and they both went flat to the ground. Dirk struck savagely, blindly. He heard the dull *crunch* of metal on bone. Slagel stiffened beneath him, then went limp.

It took a long time for Dirk to get his hands and knees above the man. He was crying without shame now, and he didn't think he could stand the pain in his left shoulder much longer. Slagel had rolled over and was lying on his belly, holding his head, moaning softly. He didn't try to rise.

"Next time," sobbed Dirk hoarsely, "use a bigger hammer."

CHAPTER
FOUR

Twenty-five years before, John Hood had staked his claim beside Hugh Glendenning's on a small creek feeding into the South Fork of the Río Cabezon. Their old cottonwood cabin still stood in the little fold of crumpled hills above the creek that had been dry since Dirk was five.

The boy halted the horse and mule he had borrowed from Acto in front of the rotting structures. He swung down, glancing at the mule behind him that carried the new shoes from San Antone, and a portable forge. He was on his way to the Keyhole as he had promised, but he had detoured to see this cabin. He was in a sullen, vindictive mood, and he shoved the sagging door in impatiently.

Why did it have to be that way? That was what he kept asking himself. First his uncle El Hood, now Dr. Alcott. Why?

The doctor's housekeeper said she had heard the *crash* from inside the house. She told everyone who would listen that she had warned the doctor a thousand times not to lean back that way in his chair. But he had been sitting out on the porch, tilting his chair back with his feet up on the railing and his pipe glowing, watching the night settle over Caprock like that for fifteen years. Somehow Dirk couldn't believe he had fallen. His neck was broken, and he was dead, and Dirk had attended the funeral this morning, but somehow he didn't think the doctor had fallen by himself.

He kept remembering that it had been fear of crossing Jess Kruger that had kept Doc Alcott from telling the true facts about the bullet causing Hugh Glendenning's death; he kept remembering that Jess Kruger had been the other man who walked into the doctor's parlor when Alcott had finally unburdened himself of the thing that had plagued him those four years, and Clyde Slagel had asked: *What's that about the frontalis, Doc?*

Dirk kicked up the puncheon flooring of the old cabin methodically. He didn't know what he expected to find. But there was a nameless connection in his mind between Hugh Glendenning's death, and Dr. Alcott's. And there was that tin box of El Hood's that had contained something John Hood had left his son. Dirk finished in the cabin, finding nothing but some old newspapers and rotting clothes and a rusty knife. When he went outside, his horse and mule were gone.

He stood there a moment, a vagrant wind whipping at his old gray coat. Then he started looking for signs. There were no other marks beside the animals' own tracks; they had drifted. He followed the trail for a mile down through the gullies that furrowed the roll of hills, coming into a level stretch of caprock. Both animals were standing there, noses muzzling the dry earth.

Dirk went over to them, tired and angry, jerking their heads up. Then he saw the hole that had been sunk in the ground. It was about two inches in diameter. There was another one farther off. Both holes had been refilled with earth. Dirk remembered Orson Glendenning had been sinking wells to find water.

"Your head ought to be bored for the holler horn," he growled at the horse, mounting stiffly. "You know there hasn't been any water around here since that creek dried up."

Grabbing the mule's lead rope, he turned around and headed back toward the cabin. He was riding from the mouth of the gully leading into the creek when his horse whinnied suddenly. There was an answering neigh from the rising ground across the creek, then a sudden scraping sound.

Dirk was pulling his reins when the shot slapped out. Lead whined viciously past him. Tossing its head, the horse took the bit and headed straight down into the bottoms. The horse bolted through scraggly mesquite in the dry creekbed, and nothing Dirk could do would stop it. He threw himself from the saddle as the next shot rang out, followed by another and another. He hit running but was going too fast to keep his balance. The mesquite *rattled* and *cracked* and tore at him as he rolled into it, trying to keep off the shoulder Victor Slagel had broken with the sledge. He stopped finally, and lay there panting, hearing his crazed horse crash up on the other bank. Then someone shouted.

"Lige, Lige. Stop it. I told you he was coming. Lige!"

"You stay there!" yelled Lige Glendenning. "That's Dirk Hood and I'm going in after him."

Dirk caught the scraping sound again. He raised himself and saw Lige Glendenning coming down the bank into the bottoms with both guns out. There were two more Keyhole hands *clattering* down the rising ground from the cabin. Dirk recognized Terry Glendenning's voice now.

"Lige, stop. Please. I won't let you."

Dirk couldn't see the girl. Lige reached the sandy bottom and plunged into the brush. Dirk squirmed around to cut away down the creek from them. He realized what they meant to do, and he was unarmed. Lige must have seen his movement. Both the man's guns began roaring, and he came on in, shouting something. Lead *clattered* through the mesquite. A bullet clipped Dirk's hat off. Another stung his hand. He turned from one side to the other, stricken with the panic of a trapped animal.

"Lige . . ." called Terry Glendenning once more, and then through the sound of Lige's bellowing guns another shot, harder, sharper. It was the last one. For a long moment Dirk crouched there, listening. There was no other sound. Finally someone came sliding down the bank.

"Dirk!" called the girl. "Come out!"

He stood straight and could see them. Lige was in the mesquite, halfway between the bank and Dirk. He was holding one gun, looking at his left hand. It was covered with blood, empty. The other gun lay at his feet. There was a surprised, blank expression in his eyes.

Terry came through the mesquite, holding a .30–30 across her stomach with both hands. A thin trickle of smoke spiraled from its bore. "I promised him you wouldn't cause any trouble," she told her brother, face pale and set. "I meant it."

Dirk broke through the mesquite toward them, feeling a dull throbbing pain in his broken shoulder from the jarring he had taken. Orson Glendenning wheeled a big black into view on the bank, spoke to one of the dismounted Keyhole hands up there. He put the horse down the barranca on its hocks and urged it through the brush to Dirk and Lige. There was a thin sound to his voice, and a hurt look in his gaunt face as he spoke to Lige.

"I never hoped to see a son of mine do a thing like that."

Lige jerked his head to his father. He opened his mouth to say something, waving his right hand vaguely toward Terry. Then he turned without speaking and walked stiffly toward the bank. Orson looked for a long moment past Dirk to where the mule had stopped and was placidly cropping mesquite, unaffected by the gunfire. Then he looked at Dirk's left arm, bent into the sling Mrs. Fowler had made from a black bandanna; his eyes dropped to Dirk's waist, unspanned by a gun belt. Finally he took a deep breath.

"One of our hands spotted you crossing the South Fork," he said heavily. "Lige got out ahead of us. Terry told me about it, but I didn't think you'd do it, Dirk. I didn't think you'd come."

"I'm a blacksmith," said Dirk. "If your horses need refitting, I'll do it."

Orson didn't speak again till a Keyhole cowhand came down the bank with Dirk's horse. Dirk mounted and got his mule. They headed toward the Keyhole house.

"What was Hugh doing in Slagel's office that day?" asked Dirk.

Orson turned toward him. "Slagel said at the trial that he'd collared Hugh and taken him to his Land Office, tried to stop him meeting you. But Hugh's wife says he went to the Land Office of his own accord."

"You own dad's old homestead site?" said Dirk.

"Of course," said Orson. "Your dad's original homestead was state land. He built the rest of his spread by buying out smaller spreads and hooking onto county land. The original survey was sort of complicated. Clyde Slagel cleared the title for us and made a new survey when he handled the deal through Hammer's bank."

"It was Clyde helping you try to locate that underground water, too, with that witch of his," said Dirk absently. "You sink any shafts over by Dad's homestead site?"

"No," said Orson. "We didn't."

"Somebody did," said Dirk.

CHAPTER
FIVE

The courthouse was a big white frame building, colonial style, with faded brown shutters. It was set back from the street on the corner of First and Mesa, directly across from Dr. Alcott's house. The sheriff had his office at the rear of the musty old building, down the hall past the courtroom. Mick Walker was in prodigious repose in his padded swivel chair, boots resting on the scarred roll-top desk. He jerked up sharply, as if he had been dozing, when Dirk came in.

"Seeco said you wanted to see me," said Dirk.

Mick shoved his hat back on his white mane, clearing his throat. "Dirk, you're letting yourself in for it, going out like you did yesterday and shoeing those Keyhole horses. And that fight with Victor Slagel. It could well constitute a violation of your parole."

"Is that why you asked me in?" said Dirk. "If Victor cracks my skull, that's all right. If I crack his, I violate my parole."

Mick swung slowly around in his swivel chair till he was looking out the window. "Jess told me he didn't send Victor out there, Dirk."

"Told *you?*" said Dirk. "Why should he bother telling you? You're his man."

"That's the point," said Mick. "Jess Kruger always shows me his cards. He lets me take care of this end, and I let him take care of his, and we don't interfere with one another. But I already know what's in his war sack before he pulls it out. And he knows what's in mine. If Jess had sent Victor out that night, I would have known it. I'm giving you that straight, Dirk."

Dirk moved to sit on the desk, staring past Mick out the window. "I'll take it straight, Mick. You never lied to me before. Maybe . . . there's been only two sides in this town for so long it just doesn't occur to us there could be a third. Somehow, I couldn't see anyone else doing it but Kruger. Mick, does a man convicted of manslaughter lose his rights of inheritance?"

"What inheritance?"

"Land."

"Didn't know you had any land."

"Supposing I did," said Dirk. "A hundred and sixty acres. A quarter-section."

"Homestead?" said Mick, turning around. "In the case of state land like that, you'd lose it by abandonment if you went to jail."

"And it would revert back to the state," said Dirk. "And anybody who wanted to could file on it. What about the original patent? Would it have to be in evidence?"

"If the new party filing on it couldn't produce the first deed," said Mick, "they'd have to go through a lot of red tape before they could get the quarter-section. What are you driving at?"

"What was in the tin box Uncle El had, for instance," said Dirk, and then turned toward the slap of boots from the outer hall. Terry Glendenning shoved open the door and ran on in, panting.

"You've got to come quick," she said, grabbing Mick Walker. "Lige just got a note from Seeco Smith to meet him on Mesa Street with his gun."

Dirk jerked off the desk, pulling her around. "Terry . . . ?"

"Yes, Dirk," she gasped, faced toward him. "The same thing all over again. You know how hot-headed Lige is. Dad couldn't stop him. I got out of the house ahead of them, but they're right behind me, Dad and Lige and the whole crew and others of the South Fork bunch. Lige'll be killed just like Hugh, and that'll only be the start of it."

Walker hoisted himself from his chair with a grunt, and the floor shook beneath his pounding weight as he went out the door. Dirk and the girl were right behind him. As soon as he reached the door behind the sheriff, Dirk could see down Mesa to where the haze of dust crawled above the cavalcade of South Forkers, just crossing Fifth Street and coming on up through the residence section. From Fifth on up to Second, Mesa Street was empty and silent. The sudden sound of Jess Kruger's shoving through the batwings of his Jaykay Saloon was startling. Behind Jess came Victor Slagel, head bandaged, walking with a painful limp.

"Jess," shouted Mickey Walker, "what's this about Seeco?"

Kruger turned a moment. "Seeco got a note from Lige Glendenning to meet him at Mesa and Second. This is it, Mick."

Mickey and Dirk and the girl had reached Kruger by then. The sheriff shoved back his hat, voice swift. "Jess, there just isn't any use in this. Glendenning's through as it is. The minute Seeco and Lige cut loose the lid'll blow. You know how it was with Dirk and Hugh. You help me stop Seeco."

Kruger looked at him, lips clamped around his cold cigar. "I thought you rode in my wagon."

Mick flushed. "You know I do. But I say there isn't any use in this. You don't have to do it to finish the South Fork bunch."

Kruger jabbed his stogie at the sheriff. "If this is the way they want it done up, that's all right by me. You handle your own team, Mick."

He turned and stamped down the sidewalk. Victor Slagel looked sullenly at Dirk a moment, hate black in his eyes, then he turned and went back into the Jaykay. The sharp *clatter* of Kruger's boots turned to a dull *thud* as he left the sidewalk and moved across the dirt in front of his barns. Seeco Smith was a dim bulk in the dusk, coming from the big double doors of the building. Mick started running after Kruger, toward Seeco.

A gust of wind eddied, sifting white dust up out of the ruts in the street, and slapped it against the curbing. It passed on down the street, and the dust settled again. Seeco Smith kept walking out toward the middle of the street. He held his fist up against his chest. Terry

Glendenning had seen that before, and Dirk heard her sharp indrawn breath beside him.

"Seeco!" called Dirk.

Smith stopped, half turning. They had been friends once, Seeco and Dirk, and the older man had taught the boy all he knew. "You aren't trying to stop me?" he asked.

"I know I can't," said Dirk. "Just tell me one thing. Did you write a note to Lige?"

"No," said Seeco, and said something else before he turned back down Mesa. "This sort of thing has always got to be done alone, Dirk, but I sort of wish you were backing me. When you went to meet Hugh Glendenning, I was backing you."

Then he turned around and moved out to the middle of Mesa and headed southward. With a curse, Mick followed him, grabbing his arm. Seeco shook him off and kept going. The dog reached the barn and turned around and around in one spot, whining softly. A pair of Kruger's Long Shank riders came out of the barn and went across Mesa behind Seeco to the hardware, taking their stand in the doorway there.

Dirk saw Lige Glendenning get off his horse at Third and Mesa. Orson leaned out of his saddle and said something to his son. Ignoring his father, Lige began walking north toward Second. Orson dismounted with a jerk, and the Keyhole crew swung down and the other South Forkers who had come. Most of them carried saddle guns. They lined out behind Lige Glendenning, moving up after him, spreading the silence before them like a rock spreading ripples in a pool.

100

Someone shoved up a window above the hardware. It made a shrieking sound. Kruger came out of the barns with his two blacksmiths and, when he saw the sheriff still arguing with Seeco, called after him angrily: "Mick, I told you . . ."

Dirk was looking up at the window of Kruger's offices on the second floor of the barns. They were bright squares of yellow light in gathering darkness. Then he looked at Hammer's bank across the street. It showed no light, top or bottom. And suddenly he knew . . . he knew!

"I'm backing you, Seeco," he breathed.

"Dirk!" called the girl.

Kruger turned sharply toward him as Dirk ran past. Then he was on the other side of Second, running down past the bank to where the San Antone Stage Company office and sheds were. He rounded the stage office to the yard behind. A solid pack-pole fence enclosed the compound, and the stables were backed up against the bank. Dirk hoisted himself over the fence with his good arm, dropped off into the compound, ran the rail till he found a coil of hemp on the middle bar. From the top rail he reached the slanting roof. He almost slid off and had to catch the edge with his left arm. The stabbing pain drew a grunt from him.

The stable roof hit the wall of the bank some four feet below the top. It cost him more agony, using his left arm to get onto the bank's roof. He kicked off his boots and ran across the tarred roof top with the rope slung on one arm. He reached the opposite parapet.

101

Peering north through the dusk, he could see Seeco Smith crossing Second. Southward, Terry Glendenning was struggling with her brother. She must have run down there while Dirk was getting on the bank's roof. He heard Orson say something, and one of the Keyhole crew grabbed the girl and pulled her over to the sidewalk.

All the time he was watching them, Dirk had been bent over the parapet. When his glance was drawn to the scraping sound to the right and below him, he held his breath. The faint dark line edging away from the brick wall might have been a gun barrel. It shifted southward, toward the Glendennings. Dirk had spotted the ventilating pipes behind him. With a swift, skilled throw he snaked the hemp around one, pulled it taut, tested it. He waited an instant longer. Seeco and Lige were less than half a block apart now, much less. And Lige spoke.

"Seeco?" he asked, and in the silence Dirk heard it plainly. He climbed onto the parapet.

"Lige," said Seeco.

Dirk knew it was the time, and his voice rang out in a violent yell as he swung down off the parapet on the rope. "Seeco!" Then his boots crashed into the rifle barrel beneath him and struck it aside just as it exploded. As he smashed on through the partly opened window, he caught a last glimpse of Lige and Seeco standing with hands gripping on their half drawn guns, faces turned up toward his shout and the sound of the shot.

102

Dirk plunged feet first into the darkened room. He struck the body of a man and crashed to the floor with glass shattering all over him, cutting at his face and neck. The man cursed beneath him, struggling to get from beneath his rolling body. Agony numbing his broken shoulder, Dirk clawed for the rifle with his good hand. The man struck at him with the rifle, gasping. Over the sharp hard scuffle, Dirk heard a rasping voice.

"Nevermore, nevermore . . ."

The man swung the rifle again, trying to knock Dirk's weight off him, and it grazed Dirk's face. Head rocking from the blow, Dirk heard someone running down the hall outside. The door shook under a man's fist.

"Unlock it!" a voice shouted. "You missed! Something went wrong and they're coming up. Unlock the door."

Dirk fought to keep on top of the struggling man beneath him. He beat blindly at him with his right fist, heard a smothered yell of pain. The rifle swung up from the side and hit him directly across the face this time, knocking him off. He felt the man scrambling away from him, heard the sharp dry sound of another shell being pumped into the chamber. Dirk threw himself upward, smashing the man back into a big square desk.

The door shook again, as if someone had thrown his body against it from the outside. The gun went off above Dirk as he fought for it, and he jerked spasmodically to the bite of hot lead across his skull. Blinded, stunned, he got a desperate grip on the barrel. Heedless of the agony in his shoulder, he held the rifle

103

with both hands and jammed it back into the man. He heard a sharp grunt, and shoved again, bending the man backward over the desk. The door buckled as the man outside threw himself at it a second time, and staggered into the room.

With a gasp, Dirk brought the rifle down squarely. The body collapsed beneath him, sliding off the desk to the floor. Unable to see the man who burst in, Dirk whirled, reversing the rifle to claw at the pump. The man shifted into the dim light from the door until half of him was silhouetted, and Dirk saw the bulk of a six-shooter in his hand, and saw the gun coming up.

"That you, Dad?" the man asked harshly.

Dirk cocked the gun without answering. The hammering detonation of both weapons filled the room.

For a long moment Dirk stood there, watching the man's body melt into the blackness of the floor. He felt the blood from his creased skull leaking down over his forehead, but that was his only wound. By the time Mickey Walker came thundering down the hall, Dirk had a lamp lit. Victor Slagel lay just within the doorway where he had taken the rifle slug. Mick stood there, pop-eyed, looking at the other man where he lay unconscious by the desk.

"Tarnation," gasped the sheriff, "Clyde Slagel."

"It's been Clyde Slagel all along," explained Dirk, after the rest of them had come up, and two Long Shank riders had carried Victor Slagel's body away. "When the North Fork began to go dry, Clyde must have realized the South Fork would go, too. He was

104

using that water-witch a long time before Orson Glendenning came and started hunting for the underground reservoir.

"No telling how many years before Dad's death it was that Clyde found the dome of water that rose beneath Dad's original homestead. Clyde sunk the shafts to verify his find. It's uncanny how thirsty animals smell water. That's what my horse and mule did out there, even though Clyde had refilled his two shafts, trying to hide them. He knew whoever owned that quarter-section would have the whip hand when the other water went."

"But your dad owned it," said Lige impatiently.

"There're always ways, with a man like Clyde," said Dirk. "When I lost the Keyhole after Dad's death, everybody took it for granted that Dad had mortgaged his original homestead along with the rest of the spread. When Clyde handled the deal, he saw on the original survey that the homestead had not been mortgaged. He cleared the title and made a new survey when Orson bought the Keyhole, and on that new survey he included the homestead site in Orson's purchase, thus covering the fact that it should have been inherited by me."

"That must have been what Hugh came to this office about, the day he was killed," said Orson. "Just a week before, I'd asked him about putting a new fence on that quarter-section. It was the first time since I'd bought the Keyhole that we'd discussed that part of it. Hugh seemed surprised I had it. He said he didn't think John

Hood would have mortgaged his original homestead under any circumstances."

Dirk nodded. "How about it, Slagel?"

Clyde Slagel sat at his desk under the watchful eye of Mick Walker; he toyed with an inkwell, nodding sullenly. "When Hugh found the homestead site was in Orson's name, he came up here asking to see the original survey. I put him off and he got suspicious. Said the next time he came he wanted it cleared up, or he'd cause trouble."

"So you sent him a note, and me a note, and waited up in your office with a rifle to make sure Hugh died whether my bullet killed him or not," said Dirk grimly. "Which it didn't."

"Two birds with one stone," said Mick Walker angrily. "Hugh dead so he couldn't spread Clyde's secret about the water. And Dirk in the pen, so Clyde could reveal his supposed mistake on the survey whenever he wanted, and have the quarter-section declared abandoned by Dirk, reverting back to the state."

"And Clyde could file on it, and have the only water in the county," said Dirk. "Only you wouldn't want a lot of red tape and investigation. You had to get the original patent. Is that what was in Uncle El's tin box?"

Slagel nodded dully. "Your father's deed and papers to the homestead. Victor had found them when your uncle came in on him."

"And Doc Alcott didn't fall off his chair by himself," said Dirk. "Did Victor take care of that, too? Because you overheard the doc tell me about a frontalis? But why this, today?"

"When Hammer refused Orson the loan," said Slagel, "Orson came up here and told me it was the finish, said to have everything straightened out for whatever would happen to his Keyhole. The homestead was still under his name, and I couldn't afford to straighten anything out or clear the papers on the Keyhole until I'd gained legal possession of that quarter-section. If Orson died, it would give me time to get the homestead site and cover what I'd done before the Keyhole was disposed of. Orson's an older man with a cooler head. If I'd sent the note to him, he might have stopped to think. I sent it to Lige, knowing Orson would come with him."

"If Dirk's bullet didn't kill Hugh," said Mick Walker, "then he was sent up on false charges and didn't legally abandon his homestead. It's yours, Dirk."

"No," said Dirk, and he was looking at Terry. "It's Caprock's, Mick. There's enough water for all of us if we use it right. As long as I've been alive, there's been fighting and hate and killing in this town over water. There won't be any more."

Clyde Slagel's crow rustled through the papers on the desk in front of its master's blank gaze.

"Nevermore," it croaked. "Nevermore."

Queen of Rustler's Range

"Queen of Rustler's Range" was Les Savage, Jr.'s original title for this story. The author was paid $200 for it on February 14, 1950. It was published under this title in *Mammoth Western* (8/50).

CHAPTER
ONE

Paul Hollister was the first to check his horse on the high ridge overlooking Nash's place. The wind boomed like a distant barrage through the dense Montana timber. It whipped Hollister's hat brim against his weathered face. It frayed the tail of his little chopping horse across its rump. It plucked strands of Raven Moore's jet-black hair from the upswept coif on her hatless head as she pulled her black stud in beside the man.

"I wish you'd let Sheriff Yale foreclose on Nash," Hollister told her. "I don't like the job."

"Yale was still out trying to come up with that rustled stock," Raven said. "Judge Manning said I was within my rights, Paul."

The autocratic tone of her voice matched the queenly look of her tall, richly formed figure in the saddle. She wore lace-up boots and fawn-colored jodhpurs that clung to the ripe curves of hips and thighs like a second skin. Bright summer sun picked up creamy highlights on the fruit-like curve of her cheeks. Hollister had been Raven Moore's foreman on the Frying Pan Ranch for a year now, and still couldn't help feeling a little breathless before the impact of her beauty.

"There's a lot of talk going on in town, Raven," he said reluctantly. "They're asking why you bothered to buy up Nash's note from the bank. His land isn't any good. His stock isn't worth sour beans."

Beneath the edges of her ducking jacket, an angry breath swelled deep breasts against a silken shirt. "Since when have you started questioning what I do, Paul?"

He met her gaze with troubled eyes. He was a big man in the saddle, with all his weight running up into his shoulders. The raw force of the elements seemed to have shaped his features. They were blunt and bold as a granite rock face, with a broad flatness through the cheek and brow. The sun had burned him dark, and the wind had weathered the flesh, till it held the graining of fine mahogany. He rubbed one flat-knuckled hand uncomfortably against Levi's so old and work-worn they had a chalky shine at the hips and knees.

"Tell me one thing, Raven. When you bought up Nash's note, did you plan on him not being able to meet the payments?"

That blank opacity had come to her eyes, the way it did whenever she got angry or stubborn. "You always stood by me before, Paul. Are you going with me now, or am I going alone?"

When he didn't answer, she wheeled in the saddle and put heels to her black. It lunged off into shale, slipping and dancing to keep upright. He held his own mare a moment, his eyes following Raven as she left the

112

shale and dropped into the meadow. The whole cañon reflected the poorness of Nash's outfit. Half his acreage had been burned over in earlier years, and fallen trunks littered the slopes with their ashen sections like the broken torsos of fallen giants. At the bottom of the cañon, Horsetail Creek plunged down from the higher peaks, the poplars shedding their cottony blossoms over it till the churning yellow water looked as if it had been sprinkled with snowflakes.

Shaking his head, Hollister gigged Peanuts off the ridge and down after Raven. He passed through meager timber and across a rock-shod meadow where gaunt cattle bearing Nash's 77 brand foraged for what poor feed remained. The cabin was set on a bench halfway down to the bottom, a trickle of smoke seeping from its cat-and-clay chimney to lose itself in shreds as soon as the wind caught it.

Raven halted her black and waited for Hollister. He drew rein and reluctantly got off. Harry Nash must have heard the *creak* of rigging. He swung the door open before Hollister could knock. He almost filled the opening, his great shoulders within an inch of touching each side of the narrow door frame. His uncut hair fell down the sides of his head in a shaggy mane, half hiding his eyes. His red wool shirt was stained with sweat and grease, and use and dirt had turned his jeans black. He brushed the hair out of his eyes, grinning ruefully.

"I guess I know what you're here for, Raven. I ain't got the money yet. Tell you what. I'll throw a cut of steers in with that road herd Alec Fox is driving to Minot . . ."

"You said that too many times before, Nash," Raven told him. "It's too late. I've come to foreclose."

The sudden anger entering Nash's face accentuated the brutal force of its heavy bones. "Seems to me being the biggest rancher in Flathead is giving you mighty ideas, Raven. You can't do this. It's Sheriff Yale's job."

"Yale is out on posse," Hollister told Nash heavily. "Raven got an order from Judge Manning."

"You still ain't got no right." A dull flush rose in Nash's thick neck till the cross-hatching of creases in its stubble-bearded flesh gleamed white as scars. "It's got to go through a court of equity. They got to sell it and give me what I got in it after you're paid off."

Raven's black eyes kindled with ironic impatience. "You ought to be a lawyer, Nash. But you wouldn't get your equity out of this, anyway. You know this outfit wouldn't bring enough money on the open market to pay off my note, much less leave you any. But I'll see that you get a fair deal. You can take your equity out in cattle. Hollister will help you gather enough to make up what you've got in the place."

Nash thrust scarred thumbs into the waistband of his jeans, leaning back. "Now, ain't that nice. Ain't that just nice."

The man was still watching Raven, but Hollister saw the slight shift of his weight, and it telegraphed his intention. Hollister knew that Nash always left his rifle leaning against the left side of the door.

114

"Get your gear and saddle up," Raven said. "We'll start right now."

"I'll do that," Nash said. "I'll do just that."

The mockery in his voice told Hollister what was coming. As Nash stepped back, his weight shifted farther to the left. Then, as he turned, he suddenly bent sideways and his arm shot out of sight behind the door frame. Hollister was already lunging for him.

Nash took a jumping step backward, giving himself enough room to swing the rifle he had snatched from against the wall. But Hollister went into him before he could swing it around. It knocked the old Henry back against Nash so that it lay horizontally between them. The barrel jumped hotly, and the sound deafened Hollister.

He let his rush carry Nash on back, going into a flimsy table and smashing it apart with their driving weight, and stumbling on through its wreckage into the bunk. Pinned against the bunk post, Nash tore the rifle from between them and raised it above Hollister's head. Before the man could smash it down, Hollister drove a punch deep into his belly.

Nash doubled forward against Hollister with a sick gasp, unable to put any force into the rifle. It struck Hollister feebly across the shoulders as it descended.

He felt Nash relinquish the rifle and heard it drop behind. He knew what was coming and tried to hit Nash again, but the man's weight came against Hollister, and he had to jump back to keep from going down. His foot caught in the wreckage of the table and he tripped backward helplessly.

115

Nash had thrown himself against Hollister blindly, incapacitated by the blow to the stomach. With Hollister's support out from in front of him, he staggered on forward. Hollister tried to roll out from under him. But Nash tripped in the wreckage, too.

His great weight crashed down on Hollister. It spread-eagled Hollister against the floor, all the air knocked from his body. Dimly he saw Nash rise up above him, saw the fist coming down. With all that was left of his will, he jerked himself aside.

Nash's fist crashed against the puncheons, and he shouted with pain. Before Nash could recover, Hollister caught his arm and used it as a lever to upset him. He rolled over with the man, smashing at his face with his free fist, and felt his fist crunch against bone.

Hollister got one foot beneath him. He caught the front of Nash's wool shirt, lifted him up, and smashed him in the jaw again. It knocked Nash back off his knee and against the wall. He remained there, half in the air, as if pinned against the logs. Then he slumped to a heap.

Hollister got to his feet. He stood amid the wreckage of the table, sucking in great breaths. His clothes were drenched with sweat, and he was trembling. But, somehow, there was no triumph in this for him. He saw that Raven had watched it from the door. There was a strange, studying expression on her face as she looked at Hollister. The violence had made no apparent impression on her.

"If you still want your equity, we'll start," she told Nash.

116

The man pulled himself to his feet, leaning against the wall, and wiped a hand down his jaw, grimacing with pain. "The hell with the equity," he said. "Take the place. You won't keep it long. You can count on that. You can sure as hell count on that."

After Nash had gone, Hollister and Raven lined out down the cañon toward the flats and the town. Hollister's whole body was beginning to ache from the fight, and he was in a bleak mood. They rode without speaking until they reached the fork at the foot of the Cabinets. They followed South Fork across a corner of Alec Fox's Cowbell toward the Flathead road. Before they reached the road, the stream had become a brackish trickle. It lifted Hollister out of his depression, puzzling him.

"I didn't realize South Fork was getting so dry," he commented.

"You've been spending too much time in the mountains," she said. "It's been coming for years. If it doesn't go bone-dry this August, it will next year. Alec Fox was a fool to settle his Cowbell down here."

"This is his only water. What'll he do?"

"Move out, I hope. There isn't another rancher around Flathead that will be sorry to see him go. I'll bet you find somebody else's brand on the inside of half his hides."

"You're letting your fight with Fox warp your thinking," Hollister said. "Nobody's ever caught him with a blotted brand. It's always been just talk."

"You don't hear that much talk without cause," she said angrily.

She kicked her horse into a run, and he gigged up Peanuts to follow her. Watching her proud, flawless seat in the saddle, he felt the poignant desires welling up again. He didn't know exactly when it was he had fallen in love with Raven. It must have been very soon after he signed on the Frying Pan. But it had torn at him for a year now. He had never felt worthy of the feeling. What could a $100-a-month ramrod offer a woman worth $100,000?

A hundred times he had been driven to tell her, and a hundred times the gap that separated them had kept him from it. He was not a shy man with women. But he had seen too many others make their bid for Raven and fail — rich men, influential men, famous men — all with far more than he had to offer. He should have broken off such a hopeless thing long ago. He had been ready to a thousand times. But each time, he had been unable to make the final break.

When he had first come to work for Raven, she had been something fine to him — a beautiful and ambitious woman who had fought her way up from the bottom, to become one of the richest ranchers in Montana. Her shrewd business sense, her courage, her driving ambition had only made her more admirable to him. But lately, that ambition had been changing, hardening, taking possession of her, till it had become something approaching greed, something that almost frightened him.

118

They reached the outskirts of Flathead, passing through the shanties that had been the first buildings here. As they passed a tar-paper and packing-crate shack, where the dirty gray wash of some sodbuster's wife hung on the sagging line, Hollister saw Raven send her covert glance at it. He had seen her do this whenever they came into town from the south, with her face hardening, and that strange mixture of bitterness and triumph filling her black eyes. And although she had never actually told him, he knew this must be the shack where she had been born.

He had heard the story in pieces. Raven's father had died when she was fourteen. She had been forced to wait on tables in town, while her mother scrubbed floors and took in washing. In this country, waitresses were still in the same category as the girls of the line, as far as the men were concerned, whether they deserved such a reputation or not. Hollister knew what that must have meant to Raven's pride.

Through the long, grueling years, she and her mother had saved enough to start an eating place of their own. With her mother's death, Raven had traded it for a shoestring outfit in the Cabinets. Those had been bitter years, too. A woman just turned twenty-one, fighting her way through the hardest winters Montana had known, holding on somehow when half the outfits in the state went under, trying to build a herd in the face of opposition from all the big outfits around her.

Whenever her opposition to the men who had fought her rise seemed too fierce, or her business deals too sharp, Hollister always sought the justifications of that

119

in her bitter past. Up till now, it had sufficed. But there was something wrong with this last deal with Nash, something insidiously wrong.

They made the turn around the Salish Hotel, and the road became Flathead's main street, passing between the false fronts of fifty buildings. A few of them had been freshly painted, but most of the siding was scaly and brown from wind and sand and weathering.

Sheriff Glenn Yale had been leaning against the support of the hotel's overhang, dragging on a smoke, but as Hollister and Raven came into view, the officer pulled the quirly from his mouth and turned to go inside. Raven drew her horse in sharply, hailing Yale. He turned back slowly. He was a lanky man in dust-grayed jeans and a cowhide vest, a wind-seamed wisdom to his sun-faded eyes.

"You didn't find my cattle?" Raven demanded.

"Nor the rustlers." He replaced the cigarette, took a drag. "We lost the tracks down by Cheyenne Butte."

"That's on Alec Fox's spread again."

Yale expelled a weary stream of smoke. "It's the badlands, too, Raven. Most of them trails end up in the badlands."

"But it crossed Fox's land."

"Yes, it did," Yale said with heavy patience. He pursed his lips around the cigarette, squinting his eyes at her. "Manning said you got a court order for Nash."

Raven leaned forward in her saddle. "Why didn't you want to serve that eviction notice, Yale?"

The sheriff held up a hand in protest. "Now, Raven . . ."

"I left you on South Fork at four o'clock yesterday afternoon," she said. "It would have only taken you three hours from there to Cheyenne Butte. Even if you slept out, you would've been back in town by the time I got here this morning. Yet Manning said you were still out. I didn't think I'd see the time when you'd side with a man like Harry Nash."

"It ain't that I'm siding with him . . ." Yale broke off, shaking his head helplessly. He dropped the smoke and ground it out with a heel. "Why do you have to be so dog-gone driving, Raven? Today, you trampled somebody none of us care much about. Tomorrow, it'll be someone we do care about. You can't keep on down this trail without getting into real trouble. I wish you'd pull up before it's too late."

Raven straightened in the saddle. "How I conduct my business is my own affair, Yale. You're the one who's going to get into trouble. You're in a public office. You shirked one of your duties today. You keep that up and there'll be a recall."

Alec Fox sauntered from the hotel as she spoke, and halted just outside the door. "Not while I'm around, Miss Moore," he said.

Raven swung sharply in the saddle to face him. Alec Fox came on over to the curb. He was a stooped, seedy man, who looked more like a farmer than a rancher, yet his Cowbell was the second largest spread in the valley. His Hyer boots were run over at the heels from more walking than a cowman usually did, and his patched linsey-woolsey jeans were caked with the dried, reddish mud of Kammas Prairies. His face, beneath the greasy

121

horse-thief hat, was formed of sharp ridges and shadowed hollows, with eyes set deep in gaunt sockets.

"Maybe you won't be strong enough to buck me when I petition for Yale's recall, Alec," Raven told him thinly.

"That why you bought Nash's outfit?" he asked. At the vague surprise in her face, Alec teetered back on his heels. "I guess you've known South Fork was going to dry up for a long time, haven't you? Nash knew it, too. He said he'd let me water my stuff in Horsetail where it crosses his pastures, if I really had to. How about you, Raven, now that you own Nash's outfit?"

"Bring back all my stock you've rustled and we might talk it over." Raven's voice was cold and cruel.

The blood drained from Alec's face. It left the flesh white as parchment across the ridge of his cheek bones and about his compressed lips. Then he took a lunging step off the sidewalk, grabbing the bit of Raven's black.

"Alec!" Yale called sharply. "No trouble."

"You'll take that back." Alec stared up at the woman. "You ain't so high and mighty you can say something like that in town and get away with it."

The black started pirouetting and trying to rear, and Raven pulled the horse back down, crying angrily at Alec: "Let him go! You know how bad he is when he's excited."

"I'm bad when I'm excited, too!" Alec shouted. "I said take that back, Raven, and I mean it."

Hollister was on the outside of the black. "Let her go, Alec!" he called, swinging Peanuts around the black's rump to get on the inside.

"The hell I will. You hear me, Raven?"

The black reared up, almost pitching Raven over its rump. Alec hung on, his face contorted, pulling the frothing snout back down again. Yale stepped off the curb, grabbing his arm. Alec swung on the horse, throwing his arm out. It slammed the sheriff across the chest. Yale staggered back, tripped on the curb, fell across the sidewalk. At the same time, Raven took the ends of the reins and whipped them across Alec's face.

Alec staggered backward, releasing the reins, his eyes squinted shut with pain. Then they flew open, and Hollister saw the savage intent in them. Hollister was on the inside of the black now. As Alec drove for his gun, Hollister put the gut hooks to Peanuts. The little chopping horse bolted right at Alec. The man's gun just cleared its holster when Peanuts charged into him. Hollister reined aside in the last instant. She veered left, her shoulder knocking Alec flat.

Hollister spun the horse back as soon as it had passed the man. Raven had succeeded in fighting the black down. He was fiddling and snorting, his snout marbled with lather. Yale had gotten to one knee on the sidewalk. Alec Fox rolled over, staring at the gun that had been knocked from his hand and was now lying six feet from him. Hollister could see that his whole body was trembling. Yale walked over and picked up the gun before Alec could rise.

"I'll keep this till you cool off," he said.

Alec got up, shaking his head. His shirt was torn across the front where Peanuts had struck him. He stared at Raven, the breath coming out of him in a shaken way. Then he looked at Hollister. "You'd better," he told Yale. "I might kill somebody."

CHAPTER
TWO

The heat of summer passed over the land, turning the aspens brown along the creek bottom and curing the buffalo grass until it curled tightly all over the high meadows.

Most of the Frying Pan stuff was in that high summer pasture, with the crew strung out through the line camps to watch it. Raven brought a pair of them down to take over Nash's cabin, making it into a line camp from which they could pasture his 77 herd. Hollister made his usual tour of the rest of the Frying Pan line camps, finding everything in order, and returned to the home ranch exactly seven days after they had met Alec Fox in town. It was late afternoon, with shadows stretched over the hot ground like tawny velvet, and a lathered horse wheezing at one of the ring posts before the Frying Pan house.

Hollister hitched Peanuts and mounted the porch. It was a big stout house with a steep shake roof, the green shutters thrown back against the immense unpeeled logs forming its walls. Through the half open front door, Hollister heard Raven's sharp voice.

"Why should they even get that far? I told one of you to keep a night watch on the fence."

The voice answering her was that of Ike Holland, one of the hands that had been put on Nash's place. "I was on night watch, Miss Moore. I'd just gone back for a cup of coffee. It was only a few minutes."

Hollister stepped through. Ike stood with Raven in front of the fireplace. He was rawhide-lean, his shotgun chaps still wet with his horse's lather, his long young face tight with worry. Raven was dressed in Levi's and the flimsiest of summer shirts that stirred silkily across the swell of breasts with each breath she took.

"You're just in time," she told Hollister. "Alec Fox has run a cut of his Cowbell stuff through our fence to Horsetail Creek. This sop-and-taters hand didn't have the guts to stop him."

Ike took his Stetson off, running fingers uncomfortably through damp yellow hair. "It wasn't that. I just didn't see any point in starting a shoot-out over a little thing like that. You know how jumpy them Foxes are. Anything's liable to set them off. It ain't as if we didn't have enough water for both outfits . . ."

"Not for a bunch of rustlers," she said. "Hollister, will you tend to this now?"

"Are you sure you want me to?" he said.

"What do you mean by that?" Her voice was sharp. Before he could answer, she turned to Ike. "Go out and saddle up a pair of fresh horses. Wait at the barn till we're ready."

Ike dipped his head, sent Hollister a furtive glance as he turned and went out. Raven followed him to the door and shut it, then turned to Hollister.

"Ike's right," he said. "After what happened in town, Alec will be primed for trouble. There'll be shooting."

"There should have been a long time ago," she said angrily.

Hollister shook his head. "That's exactly what I've tried to keep away from, Raven. I could have beat Nash with a gun out there at the shack, and I think I could have edged Alec out there in town. But when you start shooting, you're liable to kill somebody. I don't think anything is worth that. Why don't you let Alec have the water? It won't hurt you. It will ruin him if he doesn't get it."

"Paul, there's been a change in you these last weeks." She came toward him. "You haven't actually said anything, but I've felt you were critical of a lot of things I did." Her voice was deep and throaty now; she was so close her breasts nearly touched his chest. "If you didn't like the way I operate, Paul, why have you stayed on?" He took a deep breath, shaken by her nearness. But he was held from answering by the same things that had restrained him before. Finally she answered her own question. "Was it because of your feelings for me, Paul?"

"Raven . . ."

She reached up to grasp his arms. "I've thought I saw something, Paul, so many times. When we were alone together. A light in your eye. A look in your face."

He couldn't restrain himself any longer; he took her in his arms and bent his face to hers. The kiss lasted a long time. It was coolness and hotness and savage excitement and deep fulfillment all in one. When he finally drew his lips off hers, he heard the breath leave his body in a broken, shuddering way. She put her face softly against his chest, her voice muffled.

"I thought so," she said softly. "Why didn't you ever tell me before?"

"I've wanted to," he said. "Almost from the first, I've wanted to. A hundred times I've been on the verge of it. But I always came up against the same thing. What could a hundred-a-month ramrod offer a woman like you?"

"Paul," she chided gently, "when two people are in love, what each of them owns belongs to the other."

He shook his head savagely. "I tried to look at it that way, too. But no matter how you twist it, the thing comes out the same. I never did think a kept man was worth much."

"Oh, Paul, Paul . . ." There was an intense plea in her voice. "Are you going to let false pride come between us now? You've let it keep us apart for a year. Now that we've broken through, are you going to let it ruin everything?"

"Is it false pride?"

"Of course it is. Money . . ." — she made a helpless gesture around the room — "property, material holdings aren't the only things a person offers to a marriage. Not a real marriage. They're the smallest thing. You bring me something far more valuable. How long do you think I've been waiting for a man like you? A hundred men worth in dollars a hundred times as much as you have come to me. Do you think I would

128

have waited for you if a few dollars really meant anything . . . ?"

The passionate intensity of her voice, the silken warmth of her breasts against him were insidious things, crumbling his defense. And for the first time, it struck him what she was really saying. He had been so involved with his own reluctance, his own explanations that he had not stopped to realize, actually, what had happened. A great wonder leaped into his eyes.

"You're saying . . . that you feel the same way about me?"

"Of course, of course. How else can I put it? If you really love me, you'll forget all this childishness about a hundred-a-month ramrod. We're a man and woman. That's all that matters. Money comes and goes. Next winter may be so bad I'll lose everything. But we'll still be a man and woman. That's all that matters, Paul . . ."

It was as if a revelation had struck him. How right she was. How foolish he had been to let false pride stand between them for so long.

"And now that we've found each other, Paul, you won't let me down," she said passionately. "Men like Nash and Fox have tried to beat me from the beginning. They've wanted me and they've wanted my land, and they've used every dirty trick in the book to get it. They hate the idea of a woman being so big in this valley. If we let Fox have Horsetail this summer, next summer there'll be a dozen more. Our range will be so cluttered up, they can drive off half the herd and we'd never be able to stop them. I've fought alone for so long, Paul. I need somebody like you so badly. You won't let me down, now that I've found you."

He had a glimpse of that crumbling shack at the edge of town again, and the hard bitter years filling her life, and it made him feel a pain as poignant as if all the battles, all the indignities, all the insults had been his own.

"I've been wrong these past few days, Raven," he said. "Of course I won't let you down."

She gave him a last kiss. Again, he didn't know how long it lasted. He had to tear himself away. She stood in the door. When he reached the bunkhouse, he turned to see her still standing there. Her voice floated clearly to him.

"Come back, Paul. Come back to me."

Ike was waiting with a big claybank and a narrow little black. Hollister swung up on the claybank, still lost in the wonder of it. Ike stared at him, then slapped the black and bounced aboard when it bolted.

It was full night when they reached Horsetail Creek. Full night, and the moon was up in a clear sky, spilling yellow light over all the land, and the dense tamarack was sighing in the wind that never seemed to die. They reached a ridge and picked up the new fence, stretching clear across Horsetail Cañon from one ridge to the other, its wire glittering ugly as sin in the sharp light. They found Lindstrum watching the cattle, halfway up the slope, behind a boulder, mantled with buckwheat. He was a big Swede with sleepy eyes and straw-colored hair cropped short on a square head.

130

"They're still watering down there," he said. "I tried to talk with Alec, but he's sour. I didn't want to start no shooting unless you said so, Paul."

"There won't be any shooting if I can help it," Hollister said. "You follow me down to the edge of timber and stop there. A show of force will only put more gravel in Alec's craw. I'll go on down alone and talk with them."

Lindstrum rose into the saddle, and the two hands followed Hollister down to the edge of timber, where he left them. The cattle were knotted up in half a dozen different places, some of them standing to their bellies in the churning water. Then he saw the winking cigarettes in the darkness, and the pair of tall, alley-cat figures standing near a cutbank. Two horses were complacently hitched back in the silver spears of spruce trunks.

"It's Hollister!" he called. "I'm coming in."

Neither of the men moved sharply, and he realized they had already seen him and had been waiting. He rode nearer, and recognized Alec Fox and his older son Virgil. Virgil had the same slouched lines as his father, although he was broader through the shoulders. He had on a pair of shotgun chaps and a tattered Mackinaw, its padded skirts pulled back on one side to free the butt of his gun. Hollister pulled up and stepped off his horse, studying them for a moment.

"You had to cut the fence to get through, didn't you?" he said.

"You ain't putting us off," Alec said tightly.

131

Hollister drew a heavy breath. "You're making trouble for yourself you wouldn't need to, Alec."

Virgil Fox held his cigarette up to his mouth between thumb and forefinger and took a deep draw, letting the words come out with exhaled smoke. "The only trouble in this valley is having a woman like Raven Moore in it. You know as well as I do she's been trying to force us out ever since we got big enough to buck her. She had this planned 'way back. She knew South Fork was drying up. She knew the nearest water was upper Horsetail. It would ruin us if we couldn't have that."

"Sure," Alec said. "She put the pressure on the bank to get hold of Nash's note. She knew Nash couldn't meet payments if last winter was bad . . ."

"I don't want to hear all that," Hollister broke in, surprised at the savagery of his own voice. He drew a careful breath, making his voice quiet. "Listen, I came here to try and talk out a compromise. I'm sorry for what Raven said in town that day, Alec. But you've got to admit it looks bad, so many trails of the rustled stuff leading into your pastures."

"Kammas Prairies are the logical place to cross," Alec said sourly. "There ain't no market for blotted stuff to the north, and nobody's going to take it through the mountains."

"I know," Hollister said. "But you got to admit it still looks bad. If the rustling stopped, it would change Raven's attitude a lot. She'd be in a better frame of mind to talk over this water situation. Actually this feud between you and Raven has worked to the rustlers' advantage. When some of your stock is run off, Raven won't lift a hand to help. And you're as bad when some of her stuff is taken. If we'd co-operate, I think we could stop a lot of it."

"Co-operate with that witch . . ."

"Be careful what you say, Virgil."

The younger Fox grinned slyly at Hollister. "I always thought you looked sort of moon-eyed when you was around her. Been cutting a rusty with Raven all this time, and I'll bet she don't even know it yet."

A little pucker of muscle ran through Hollister's cheek. "I'm trying to give you a chance here, Virgil. You've cut a fence. You're trespassing. If you'll get off peaceable, I'll try to work something out so you can use this water."

"You can't work anything out with Raven," Alec said. "We've tried it before. And we ain't getting out. Those cattle will die if they go another day without water."

"If you won't talk it over, you're getting out."

"You ain't making us."

"I'll drive those steers back myself." Hollister whirled for his horse, in an anger of his own at their stubbornness. He caught up the reins and swung them over the claybank's head, lifting his left foot to the stirrup. Virgil jumped after him, grabbing his shoulder and trying to pull him back.

"You ain't touching them cattle!"

Almost pulled off his feet, his foot in the stirrup, Hollister swung his free arm against Virgil, catching the collar of his coat and shoving him viciously backward. Virgil tripped and went down. Before the man had struck the earth, Hollister saw Alec Fox's whipping motion, heard him shout.

"I told you, Hollister . . ."

Hollister was hanging onto the reins of the plunging horse, his foot still caught in the stirrup, and had to draw that way. He threw himself against the animal for support and pulled. The next thing he knew, his gun was making a deafening roar and kicking upward. He saw that Alec had his gun out, but it was not pointed at Hollister yet. The man's mouth opened in a surprised way. Then he dropped the gun, clutched at his thigh with both hands, and pitched forward on his face.

At the same time, there was the *crash* of another gun. Sand kicked up a foot from Hollister. The fighting horse screamed and reared. Hollister had to let go the reins and tear his foot from the stirrup to keep from being taken off his other foot, and he fell away. He came up on his belly with his feet in the water, and heard Lindstrum's voice.

"Don't shoot again, Leo. I'm behind you, and I'll cut you in two if you do." There was a moment of intense silence. Virgil Fox had sat up. He remained that way, staring with parted lips up into the timber. Then Lindstrum spoke again, from the trees above: "Now, drop that saddle gun, Leo. Stand up and walk down there."

Both Hollister and Virgil watched tensely till the first man appeared from the black-shadowed timber. He was Leo Fox, the younger son of Alec. Only twenty, he had the same wolfish body, long and slack. Pine needles still clung to the front of his tattered Levi's and greasy

Mackinaw, where he had been lying on the ground. There was a three-days' growth of tawny beard on his narrow jaw, and his eyes glowed like coals from the shadow beneath his hat brim. In a moment, Lindstrum came tailing him, Winchester crooked in one elbow.

"They had him staked out up there behind a boulder, Paul," the Swede said. "I spotted him before the shooting started. I'm sorry he got in that first shot."

"You did all right, Lindstrum," Hollister said, getting to his feet.

Virgil rose, too. He sent one hate-filled glance at Hollister, then walked over to his father. Leo came down to Alec, too, ignoring the threat of Lindstrum's gun. The two boys knelt beside their father, turning him over gently. Alec lay with his head thrown back in the sand, his eyes shut in pain. His pants leg was sodden with blood. Hollister suddenly felt sick at his stomach. He tore off his bandanna.

"Looks like it hit an artery. We'd better get a tourniquet. Lindstrum, ride to Flathead for the doc . . ."

"Don't touch him," Virgil snarled. The terrible savagery in his face, turned up to Hollister, stopped him. Hollister stood helplessly holding his bandanna while Virgil tore off his own neckerchief and knotted it high about his father's thigh. "Can you get on your horse, Pa?" he said.

Alec's voice came feebly. "I don't know, Son. I'm so dizzy."

"You can't make him ride," Hollister said. "He's too weak from loss of blood."

135

"We ain't leaving him here with you wolves," Virgil said. He rose, turning to Hollister. "If Pa dies, Hollister, I'm coming after you. There ain't nothing on God's green earth that will stop me. I'll come after you and I'll get you. If it's the last thing that happens in this world, I'll get you."

CHAPTER
THREE

Hollister got back to the Frying Pan after midnight. A light still burned in the parlor, and he drew up the claybank by the ring posts and ground-haltered there. Nobody answered his knock, and he swung the door part way open to look in. The door *squeaked*, and through the growing crack he saw Raven start up suddenly on the couch. She stared blankly at the door, then relaxed.

"I guess I dozed off." She smiled. "Did you send them packing?"

"I thought I could do it without trouble," he said. "I couldn't. Alec got hit bad."

He saw compassion pass through her face for an instant, then it seemed as if she blotted it out deliberately. "That's too bad," she said. Her quilted satin housecoat shimmered across the ripe curves of her body as she rose. "Did you get the cattle off?"

He stared at her. "Is that all that matters?"

"Is there any use wasting sympathy on Alec?" she asked. "I know you wouldn't shoot unless he drove you to it." She came toward him, smiling triumphantly. "The Cowbell won't last a week without water. Alec is through. This rustling will stop, and Yale won't have

137

them behind him next election. I can get a decent man in office."

He stared at her, a strange sickness growing in him. "Alec is probably bleeding to death on his way home right now. And all you do is stand there and figure out how much more power it will give you in the valley. You said money or property or power didn't matter. Yet, you're willing to kill for it."

"I said money didn't matter when it came to us, Paul."

"If it matters this much, it will matter between us. What'll you ask me to do next, Raven? If the sheriff gets elected anyway, will you set it up so I have to shoot it out with him?"

Lamplight flickered through the angry toss of her black curls. "Paul, don't be a fool . . ."

He stepped back sharply as she moved toward him. "You did that before," he said. "I was so dizzy with you the last time I left here, I believed everything you said. I thought they were all against you. I thought you were only fighting for what was yours. But it's the other way around, isn't it? Maybe it started that way, but now you're on top. Power's gone to your head, Raven. It's twisted you. I should have seen that a long time ago. But I guess I didn't want to. Does love blind a man that much?" He shook his head. "I shouldn't ask you. You don't know what love is."

"Paul, I do . . ." Her voice sounded hysterical; she caught his arm, trying to keep him from turning out the door. "I meant what I said. That was real. I do love you."

138

"I meant what I said, too." He tore loose of her. "Only I was right the first time. What could a hundred-a-month ramrod offer a woman like you?"

"You're not going?"

"I'm not staying."

He got aboard the claybank and heard her call and didn't turn around. He went down to the bunkhouse and got his bedroll and switched his saddle onto Peanuts and left. It was too late to reach town unless he wanted to ride all night. The nearest cabin was Nash's place. Ike and Lindstrum had been two of his closest friends on the Frying Pan, so he headed there. He got there about 3:00 in the morning, found the big Swede riding the fence at the foot of the cañon, and told him he was turning in without saying anything about what had happened at the main house.

Hollister woke to sun streaming against his face and the smell of bacon grease and strong coffee. Ike was in his long red underwear and his Stetson at the cook stove, forking strips of bacon from the pan. Lindstrum sat on another bunk, cuddling a cup of coffee, eyes bleary from his night watch.

"I'll pour some black-strap in this bacon grease and we'll have Charlie Taylor for our pan bread." Ike grinned. "Raven send you back, Paul?"

Hollister swung his legs to the floor and sat up, running fingers through his short curly hair. "Yeah," he said.

The Swede squinted at him over the steaming cup. "Or maybe you and her had an argument over what happened last night, huh?"

Hollister raised his eyes to them. They were both watching him now. There was a knowledge beyond his years in the wind-crinkling at the corner of Ike's blue eyes.

"We think she's getting pretty high-handed too, Paul," the blond boy said. "Maybe you can't fight as long as she has without getting hard. She's changing, isn't she?"

Hollister lowered his head wearily, reaching down for a boot. "I quit last night," he said.

For a long space, there was no sound except the *crackling* bacon grease. Finally Lindstrum's tin cup *clanked* dully as he set it down.

"That's too bad," he said emptily.

Hollister got his boots on and stood up, and saw the look in their eyes, half pleading, half apologetic. He grinned thinly. "It isn't as bad as that. And don't think you have to quit just because I did. I know there isn't another spread in a hundred miles would hire a Frying Pan man. She's fought them all too bitterly."

Ike turned back to his cooking. "I guess I won't bother making that Charlie Taylor after all," he said disconsolately.

CHAPTER
FOUR

They ate a silent breakfast, and then Ike dressed and dragged a couple of running irons and a stamping iron with the Frying Pan brand from beneath the bunk. "We got to finish venting Nash's Seventy-Seven stuff, Paul. You stay here if you want."

Hollister looked at the running irons. "Didn't Nash leave you his stamping iron?"

"I don't think he was using one," Lindstrum said. "His Seventy-Seven mark varies too much from cow to cow."

"But it's an awful good piece of drawing," Ike said. "He's had a lot of experience somewhere."

It stayed in Hollister's mind after they left. He went out to get water from the stream, thinking about it all the time. He came back and used Ike's cracked mirror to shave by. He had just finished this when he looked out the door and saw the horse climbing to the bench. It was Raven, on her black. He had never seen a horse so beat. She looked as done in. Her hair was torn free by the wind and curled wildly about a pale face. Her ducking jacket and jeans were white with dust. She hauled the lathered animal up hard, staring down at him.

"You cooled off?"

It was like a dull, throbbing pain away down in him even to look at her again, knowing it was over for good. "No," he said. "I told you."

"Paul, I need your help. The Foxes hit the herds up by Sun Rim a couple of hours after you left last night. One of the hands from the Sun Rim line camp came down to tell me."

"How do you know it was the Foxes?"

"Who else could it be? They're getting back at me. You can see that. I rode for Sheriff Yale and got him on the trail before dawn. The tracks cut down through Kammas Prairies just like they always do. So close to the Foxes that we only had to cut a mile away from the trail of the rustled stock to reach the Cowbell house. The Foxes were there. They wouldn't let Yale near. They started shooting and finally made a run for it. Yale wouldn't follow them. He said he didn't have anything on them. He and the posse followed the rustled stock on down toward the badlands. But I trailed the Foxes. They headed toward these mountains, Paul. Right into the Cabinets."

"What does that prove?"

"I've been thinking, Paul. Nobody's ever followed a trail through those badlands. Even the Indians lose it. We've always taken it for granted the rustlers were running on south for the markets down there. But they could head west, into these mountains, as soon as they got in the badlands."

"Why? It would take them weeks to get through to the markets on the other side. No rustler's going to haul a hot brand that long."

"Maybe they don't take it to any market," she said. "Maybe they just change the brand and hold it till the scar heals. If the new brand is registered, they're safe."

"You're thinking of the Cowbell again," he told her. "What about the Seventy-Seven?"

"Nobody could change my Frying Pan into a Seventy-Seven."

"Nash was using a running iron. Ike said it was an awful good job of drawing."

She swung down. "That still doesn't hold water. It's the Cowbell, Paul. You know the talk it caused when Fox first registered. Only a few minor changes and it's a Frying Pan. Please, Paul . . ."

She stepped in close, arms circling his neck. For a moment, he gave in to the softness of her body, the heat of her lips. Then he tore loose, holding her at arm's length.

"No. You won't do that to me again. You mix me up so much I think you're right, Raven. You won't make me kill a man for you when I don't think he's guilty of anything."

"Alec isn't dead, Paul. He was riding with his two boys."

He stared at her, a surge of relief filling him so poignantly it was almost pain. He saw the triumph fill her eyes, and realized she had been holding it till last.

"Now . . . will you help me?"

"You miss the whole point, don't you? A foot higher and I would have killed Alec. And you sent me out to do it."

A heated flush filled her face. Then she wheeled and swung aboard the black, wheeling it broadside so he could see the Winchester booted under her left stirrup leather.

"Then I'm going myself." She almost sobbed it. "They won't get away with this. Just because I'm a woman. They won't!"

She spurred the horse into a run down the cañon. His whole body cried out to follow. But his mind said he'd be the worst kind of fool to let her rope him in again. He went back into the shack and sat down on the bunk. The broad planes of his face were bleak and flat, his long lips were compressed so tightly there was a ridge of white flesh at their edges. She would go after them, all right. She was that kind. And she'd fight for what she thought was right if she came up with them. And they'd fight back. It could well be Raven who got hit. Who got killed.

He rose from the bunk, unable to bear the thought. He went out and saddled up, lashing his booted saddle gun under the stirrup leather. He lined out down the cañon, taking an hour to reach the edge of Kammas Prairies. He had not picked up sight of Raven yet, but her trail was plain. It followed the edge of the Prairies southward till it reached the area the Fox men would cross if they came straight into the mountains from their house. Hollister found where Raven had dismounted, trying to pick up their trail. Finally she had found it, and headed into the mountains after it. She had worked cattle herself enough to be a good trailer.

144

Now her tracks, mingled with that of the Foxes, led Hollister deep into the Cabinets. Afternoon waned and dropped heavy shadows down rock-shod slopes, and the timber boomed in the wind. He pushed Peanuts hard, eyes aching from studying sign so long.

CHAPTER
FIVE

Darkness came on him in a deep cañon. He made the mistake of trying to follow the trail before the moon rose. He followed the tracks into a thick stand of buckwheat and scrub oak. It had been leading out of the cañon toward the ridge so he guessed it was going on over the ridge, and followed this line of direction. He lost it in the talus on top, and crossed this and sought it on the other slope. He couldn't find it. Pushed by a terrible urgency, he resorted to guessing. The Foxes had been pushing hard. They would know that a horse wore out faster on the slant of a slope than a cañon bottom. So they'd go down again.

He dropped into the cañon bottom. Finally he found the pocking of prints in some mud banking a creek. He followed it on upcañon. Then the moon came out and showed him he was on the wrong trail. The tracks were more pointed than a horse's, and had no shoes. They were a bunch of steers being driven into the mountains.

He halted here, with the wind sighing about him. Was this the Foxes? Had they known the cattle were here? There must have been a reason for their heading so directly for this point. Unable to reach a final decision, he thought of circling back and finding the other trail. But he knew he might lose this one by that. And lose time. Too much time. He had to reach Raven before she came up with the Foxes. He didn't even want to think about what might happen if he didn't.

The cañon was narrow, rock-walled, and the only course the driven cattle could have taken was along its bottom. So he ceased following their tracks and pushed Peanuts as hard as she would go. Finally the cañon came to a stop, with the dead end built into great benches that looked as if they finally leveled off in a plateau. The rise was so tumbled and broken here that it did not present much difficulty in ascending. He found the cattle prints again and followed the switchbacked trail they had taken up. He reached the plateau with Peanuts blowing and shaking beneath him. The flat was grassed over, stretching off toward the real peaks of the Cabinets. Their rock faces flashed like titanic jewels in the moonlight, and their snowfields glittered like marble meadows. He pushed across the plateau, through scrub timber, coming abruptly to the edge of the precipice.

Some former upheaval had cut a slash clear across the plateau, forming a shallow cañon, its sheer walls broken here and there by erosion into talus fissures that slid off at steep angles. From the brush at its bottom came the furtive yellow gleam of a fire, the soft bawl of cattle.

Hollister found the trail the cattle had taken down, one of those eroded gullies, cutting into the cliff at an angle just slanted enough so an animal could keep its feet. It was deep in shale and talus, however, and, once in it, a man would start a minor avalanche if he pulled his horse up. Peanuts danced like a circus horse, trying to keep her feet on the treacherous surface. He was far enough away so that his approach would not be seen or heard by whoever was at the fire.

Two-thirds of the way down, however, he reached a bench, overgrown with willow and oak, and thought it safest to leave his horse hitched here. He got his Spencer falling-block from the saddle boot and made the rest of the way down on foot. He had just reached the base of the cliff, seeking cover in the thimbleberry here, when a horse by the fire whinnied. He could see the man at the fire straighten up suddenly from a hog-tied cow he had been branding. Firelight illuminated his face. It was Harry Nash.

"Never mind, Nash." It was Raven's voice, coming clearly to Hollister. "I've got you covered."

From shadows farther down the cañon, Raven rode her black into the circle of light from the fire, holding her Winchester on Nash. Hollister realized that she, too, must have lost the Foxes' trail in the darkness, and, losing her way in the maze of cañons leading to the plateau, she had somehow come upon another entrance to this gorge.

"Where are the Foxes?" she asked Nash.

There was a puzzled anger to the man's voice. "The Foxes?"

Hollister had the impulse to call out, to show himself. But he checked it, knowing that might distract Raven's attention enough for Nash to get her. Raven got off her horse, still holding the gun on Nash, and moved over to stare at the hog-tied steer.

"You're changing my Frying Pan into a Seventy-Seven," she said.

He laughed. "Didn't you think it could be done?"

She looked up at Nash sharply, and Hollister was near enough to see the surprise in her face. Before she spoke, however, a cry rang from the bluff behind Hollister.

"Nash, is that you by the fire? We're fed up with playing it straight. Raven set Yale and his posse on us. They'd've lynched us sure. We're coming in."

Raven half turned at the voice. An involuntary shout left Hollister. But it was too late. Nash was already lunging at the woman. She tried to whip back and bring her rifle to bear. Nash knocked it aside as it went off, and crashed into Raven. The weight of him knocked the woman over, and Nash tore the rifle from her hands as she fell.

"Nash?" It was Virgil Fox's voice. "What you shooting at?"

"It's all right!" Nash yelled. "Come on in! I've got Raven right here!"

With a wild whoop, the Foxes put their horses over the lip and came sliding down the gully. Hollister was off to one side of its mouth, in the brush, but he knew he had to get Raven out of this before they hit the bottom and piled up the odds against him.

"It's Hollister, Nash!" he shouted. "Drop your gun! I've got mine covering you!"

Instead of dropping it, Nash lunged for the darkness outside the circle of firelight, snapping a shot at Hollister's voice as he did so. The bullet rattled through brush six feet from Hollister. He fired at Nash and saw the man jerk and go to one knee, still holding Raven's gun. At the same time, Raven had scrambled to her feet and was running out of the light. Still on his knee, Nash wheeled, lifting the rifle toward Raven.

A great fear drove Hollister to his feet. He snapped the finger lever down on his falling-block and fired, and snapped it down again and fired and kept it up till his gun was empty, and Nash lay sprawled on his belly, motionless. When the echoes died, and Hollister came out of the frenzy, he heard the Foxes shouting at their horses. He wheeled back to see that they had made the mistake of trying to stop when the shooting began. They had put their animals over the rim at a hard clip, and, when they had tried to pull up, the slippery shale beneath the horses took their hoofs out from under them. The two behind had already slid into the leader. For an instant the three animals danced down the steep gully, fighting to keep from falling, bunched together. Then they went down.

Hollister saw one rider dive off his animal into the brush at the side. A second slid off his horse's rump into the shale. The third went with the horses. Slipping, sliding, flopping over and over, they went on down. They hit the bottom in a screaming tangle. Two of the horses scrambled up, whinnying wildly, but the third lay motionless, pinning the man. For a moment, with

150

the dust settling, there was no sound. Then the man began to stir under the horse.

"Virgil," he moaned feebly. "I can't get out. Come and help me, Son . . ."

Without thought, Hollister broke from the brush toward him. There was the *crash* of a shot. He dived back into cover with the bullet kicking up dirt a foot from him.

"Stay away from him, Hollister." It was Virgil's screaming voice, from the slope above. "You ain't killing Dad while he's helpless."

"Virgil!" Hollister shouted hoarsely. "Don't be a fool!"

A second shot cut him off, searching him out in the thimbleberry. Through the foliage, he could see the rider who had slid off the rump of his horse. He was lying in the shale of the gully, halfway up the slope, and he rolled up to an elbow, shaking his head.

"Leo!" Virgil shouted at him. "Get into them bushes! Hollister's down there! He'll kill you sure as hell!"

Leo raised his head, casting a dazed look toward the bottom of the cliff. Then he began scrambling for the brush. Alec began moaning again, where he lay beneath the horse.

Then Raven's voice came from the cover of brush and darkness beyond the fire. "Virgil, you can't leave your father out there. He's in pain."

"Dad," shouted Virgil, "can't you get out? They'll kill us if we show ourselves!"

Alec made a feeble effort to pull himself from beneath the dead horse, then sagged back to the ground.

Raven called again: "Virgil, we won't kill you, it's all over! I was wrong. I see that now. It was Nash running off our stuff all the time. When I first saw that, and knew I'd almost killed Alec for what Nash did, I realized how wrong I'd been about everything. I realized how twisted my values had become. I admit I planned the Horsetail deal from the first, Virgil. I knew South Fork was drying up. I knew there was a chance Nash couldn't meet his note. I knew I could keep you from water if I got hold of the Seventy-Seven, and you'd be forced out. But it's over now. You can use Horsetail Creek whenever you want. We'll sign Nash's Seventy-Seven stuff over to you for the cattle you've lost."

"You're wasting your breath, Raven!" Virgil's voice sounded wild. "We've fallen for too many of your tricks before."

"Virgil, you can't leave your dad out there in pain . . ." Raven's voice broke. "Oh, how can I show you . . . ?"

She stopped suddenly, there was a pause, then a rustle of brush from over there. Hollister's breath clogged up in him as he realized what it meant.

"Raven!" he shouted. "Don't!"

She appeared as a shadowy figure, at first, beyond the firelight. She passed Nash, not looking down at him, a great strain graven into her face.

"Get back, Raven!" screamed Virgil. "I'll kill you."

"It's over," she answered. "I've got to prove that to you. We can't leave Alec lying there."

152

The shot smashed into her voice. Dirt spewed up in front of Raven, splattering her jeans. She halted sharply, hung there a moment, white-faced. Then she moved on.

"I'll kill you!" Virgil shouted. His voice was high-pitched and frenzied. "Stop, Raven. The next one will be through you."

She kept on walking. Hollister had stopped breathing. Soundless tears ran down his cheeks as he realized he was helpless to stop her or aid her in any way. He had pulled his six-gun, but he knew a single shot from him would set Virgil off again for good. A strange, poignant pain filled him. Raven kept on walking. That was the only sound. Her boots *crunching* into the rocky soil. One after the other. A shudder ran through Hollister's body.

Then she reached Alec Fox.

She bent down and put her shoulder against the horse, tugging, pulling, shoving it off the man. Finally he was free. She sat down beside him and took Alec's head in her lap.

A moment after that, Hollister saw Virgil come to his feet in the brush on the slope. Leo appeared, farther down. Neither of them spoke. Slowly both of them started down through the bushes toward the bottom. In Raven's tear-stained face, Hollister could see the same compassion he had seen for a moment when he had first told her Alec was shot. It was like a revelation to him. The three men silently converged on those two figures on the ground, and stopped, and stood looking down at them.

"It looks like his legs were out flat when the horse fell on them," Raven said softly. "I don't think they're broken. You ride for the doctor, Leo. It'll be on my bill."

Leo looked at Virgil, and Virgil nodded, still staring at Raven. "Go ahead. I think it's all right now."

Raven was still looking up at them, a plea in her face. "Can you ever forgive me? Any of you? I thought I was doing right. I thought I was fighting for what was mine. It had been so hard. Ever since I was a little kid, it's been so hard." She looked at Hollister. "You were right, Paul. Power had gone to my head. It took this to make me see it."

"All that matters is you do see it," he said.

"I suppose it would be too much to ask you to come back, Paul."

"I'm already back, if you want me."

"I want you, Paul." Her voice was husky. "More than anything else. And this time, I do mean it."

"This time" — he smiled — "I believe you."

Arizona Showdown

With most pulp magazines discontinuing publication, the digest-sized *Zane Grey's Western Magazine* published by Dell Publishing was an anomaly since it was, for a time at least, highly successful. A short novel like "Arizona Showdown" earned the author $1,000 upon acceptance.

CHAPTER
ONE

It was good to ride into your home town this way. Good to smell the hot spring dust stirred up by your buggy wheels. Good to know there would be a friend on every corner, a bottle and a game waiting at the Black Jack, a dozen of the prettiest girls in Arizona to choose from when you got tired of cards. And the first friend to appear was Charlie Casket, stepping out of a lunchroom and letting the deck appear like magic in his slender fingers.

"Pick a card, Brian."

"Five minutes, Charlie. Got to hit the bank."

And then the barber, coming out of his door. "Looks like a shave this morning, Mister Sheridan."

"Around eleven, Eddie. Got to drink my breakfast first."

And the hostler, standing in front of his stables. "Better let me rub them bays down, Mister Sheridan. Ain't fittin' the biggest man in Apache Wells gets pulled around by a couple of dusty rumps."

Before Brian Sheridan could answer, the banker's kid cut around a corner and ran toward the buggy. His eyes were round as silver dollars and the fear on his white face wiped the grin off Sheridan's mouth. The boy caught the side of the buggy with a freckled hand, running alongside.

"The Gillettes are in town," he panted. "They're lookin' for you and they've all got their guns."

Sheridan frowned sharply at the boy, then pulled a quarter from his pocket and flipped it to him. "Thanks, Dee. You better go home now."

Sheridan drove the half block to the bank at a walk, noting how quiet the town suddenly seemed. There was no movement in the street ahead of him. The adobe walls and squalid false fronts ran down to the little sunlit plaza like sour, scowling faces, gaping blankly at him from the eyeless sockets of shadow-black doors and windows.

Sheridan tried to shake off the apprehension. He had pacified the Gillettes before. What the hell was wrong with him? At the two-story frame building housing the bank, he stepped out of the buggy, winding the reins around the whip stock. Then he moved up onto the plank sidewalk, a tall red-haired man with all the temper of the red Irish flashing in his blue eyes and all their irrepressible humor curling at his lips. He had a taste for bottle-green frock coats and wore a hat for every day in the week. This was his Wednesday Stetson, bone-white and freshly blocked, the one he always wore with his white silk cravat and bench-made boots of red Morocco.

Before he reached the bank door, he saw three people come out of Jess Miller's Mercantile directly across the street. It was Pa Gillette and his two sons, Cameron and Asa. Their faces were white and set.

"'Morning, Gillette." Sheridan smiled. "Your beef getting fatter on that new forty?"

There was no answer. The three men kept walking toward him. Pa Gillette was one of the small-time ranchers from the Salt River section, a big, gnarled man whose face was seamed and furrowed like a haphazardly plowed field. He wore blue jeans held up by a single gallus, so ingrained with dirt and filth they looked black.

Behind him, moving ponderously, came Cameron, an immense blond man with hair like straw thatching. Asa, the younger son, brought up the rear, a nervous, driven boy with hollow cheeks and feverish eyes.

Sheridan felt his face tighten as they stopped in front of him and stood there, staring at him in silence.

Then Pa Gillette said: "Guess you'll be the richest man in Gila County now."

Sheridan frowned at him. "How do you mean?"

"Asa wanted to shoot you," Pa said. Anger shook his voice. "I told him they'd hang us for that."

"They can't hang us for whipping the hell out of you," Asa said.

Sudden anger cut through Sheridan. "What the hell for? I don't know what you're talking about, Pa."

"Morton Forge was always getting into some kind of trouble," Pa Gillette said thickly. "When you foreclosed on him, I thought maybe you was in the right. I even kept quiet when you shut down Partridge's outfit. He wanted to get up a bunch of us and burn you out. He said you was a damn' octopus, eating us up. I wouldn't believe him. But you was just stringing us

159

along till you really had us over a barrel, wasn't you? Tellin' us we could go ahead and buy that forty acres, you wouldn't call the note this time. Letting us stretch out so thin we couldn't ever get back."

"Are you saying . . . ?"

"You know what happened!" Pa almost shouted. He lunged forward to hook Sheridan's coat with one hand, pulling him up on his toes. His voice broke with his rage and his eyes were blazing. "Your foreman was with the deputy sheriff when he brought the notice this morning."

Sheridan grabbed the man's arm, trying to twist free. "Let go, Pa. I didn't send out the law."

Still holding his coat, Pa shoved Sheridan so hard he had to stumble back against the wall of the building to retain his feet.

"You can stand there and say that?" Pa shouted in his face.

"An hour ago Cline's deputy was on my door stoop and that damn' Latigo with him."

"But I didn't send him!" Sheridan was shouting in a hot anger of his own now. He got purchase against the wall and thrust all his weight into Pa, shoving him back off balance and tearing free at the same time. He heard his coat rip. Pa tried to come back in at him, but Sheridan twisted free.

"Don't let him get away!" Asa shouted.

Sheridan had a blurred impression of Cameron coming into him. He tried to dodge aside. But the man's great body smashed him back against the wall. He saw Cameron pull back a rope-scarred fist — saw

160

Pa Gillette lunging back in from the other side — knew he'd be finished if they both caught him there.

He dropped to his knees as Cameron struck. The man's fist cracked into the wall above Sheridan's descending head. Then he drove outward against the man, waist high. It carried Cameron across the sidewalk and he pitched off the curb with Sheridan sprawling out on top of him.

He tried to roll off Cameron but both Pa and Asa lit on him from behind. He went back down beneath a rain of blows and kicks. Stunned by it, he had a blurred vision of a booted leg, and twisted around to catch it and throw his weight against it. This toppled Pa back into Asa and both of them went down.

Sheridan went right with them. He saw Asa's face before him as the man tried to twist free and rise. He smashed it squarely with all his weight behind the blow. Blood spurted and Asa went flat on his back against the street.

Sheridan was still partly on top of Pa. The elder Gillette twisted up into him, jamming a knee in the crotch. The pain of it made Sheridan double helplessly over on the man.

Pa clawed at him, trying to get out from beneath. In desperation, Sheridan pawed for some handhold. His fingers found Pa's hair. Pa clawed at his eyes and tried to knee him again. Face still twisted with pain from that first knee, Sheridan slammed Pa's head against the ground. He was dimly aware of Asa rolling over, face whipped by rage.

161

"He's killin' Pa!" Asa bawled. There was no reason left in the wild tone of his voice. With all the thoughtless impulses of his hot rage twisting his face, he went for his gun.

Sheridan let go of Pa's hair, rising up on the man, filled with the helplessness of knowing what was coming and being utterly unable to stop it. Asa's gun was clearly out before the girl's figure blocked him off, jumping down into the street.

"You can't kill him in cold blood! Asa, you can't!" she cried.

Sheridan saw Asa jump to his feet, trying to lunge aside so she would not block him off. But she threw herself into him, grabbing for the gun arm and hanging on, fighting with him till he finally stopped.

Sheridan tried to get up off the half-conscious Pa, but he was too drained to gain his feet. He had to crawl to the curb and hoist himself to a sitting position. The air passed in and out of him in great, broken gusts. Each breath was stabbing pain. At last, with a great effort, he lifted his head, to see the girl still standing in front of Asa, her head turned over one shoulder to look at Sheridan.

"Thanks, Estelle," he said. "I think Asa really meant to kill me."

"Nobody would have been killed," George Wolffe said, from behind Sheridan. "Unless it was Asa."

Sheridan turned to see Wolffe standing by the bank door, a gun in his hand. He was a tall man, broad-girthed and solid in his claw-hammer coat and homespun jeans. His square face was Indian-dark

162

beneath a flat-topped black hat, and his eyes were fixing their black intensity on Asa Gillette.

"I was in the Black Jack when I heard the commotion, Brian," he told Sheridan. "I wish I could've gotten here sooner."

Sheridan winced as his grin pulled at cut lips. "Soon enough, George. Folks'll start saying you're my bodyguard instead of my business manager. Where does a lawyer get off packing a smoke pole that big?"

Wolffe looked down at the immense Frontier Colt he held, and then raised his eyes again, unsmiling. Estelle Gillette had finally turned from her brother now. She was a richly formed girl in simple blue calico, her hazel eyes flecked with little lights as tawny as her honey-colored hair. There was a pouting ripeness to her underlip as she watched silently while her father gained his feet.

Cameron was already erect, shaking his straw-thatched head from side to side like a bull with blowflies. Pa's whole face was still squinted up with pain, but it could not obscure the implacable anger glittering in his sun-faded eyes.

"This ain't the finish," he said. His voice was guttural with rage and frustration. "You better stay indoors after this, Sheridan. You'll be taking your life in your hands to put one foot outside. There won't be a road safe for you to ride in all Arizona."

He turned and stalked off, gesturing for his clan to follow. Cameron followed, and it left only Estelle, standing in the street, staring at Sheridan with tortured eyes. He got shakily to his feet, holding out one hand.

163

"Estelle, surely you don't believe . . . ?"

"I don't want you to speak to me," she said. "Ever again."

After the Gillettes had left, Sheridan turned into the bank. At the door he grew so dizzy he had to lean against the frame. His face was putty-colored with sickness.

"You're really out of shape," George Wolffe said. "Little fight like that."

Sheridan laughed shakily. "Have to get in some more riding, I guess."

"I'm sorry about the girl."

"They come and go."

"I thought you were really interested in Estelle."

Sheridan glanced at him, seeing a sharp calculation in his eyes. "You manage my money, George," he said. "I'll take care of my love life." He turned squarely to Wolffe. "That was sort of a dirty trick, wasn't it? I'd given Pa my word we wouldn't push that note till he could get this new forty paid off."

Wolffe frowned at him. "I didn't know that."

"How can you say that, George? I told you the other night after the party."

Wolffe's frown deepened. "I don't remember. Are you sure, Brian? You were pretty drunk that night."

Sheridan squinted, trying to recall. Then he shook his head helplessly. "I can't remember, either. If I didn't tell you, I sure made a mess of things."

Wolffe put a hand on his arm. "It doesn't matter. If you'd take any interest in the politics of this town,

164

you'd know the Gillettes had to be put out of the way anyhow. Under Pa's leadership, the Salt River bunch is stronger than ever. They've been trying to pull you down for years."

"This goes beyond politics, George," Sheridan said. "I gave Pa Gillette my word. He trusted me and took out a second mortgage to get that Donovan pasture. You know he can't raise the money to meet our note under those circumstances."

"It just shows you how stupid the whole thing has gotten. Two men whose parties have fought for years trusting each other."

Sheridan flushed. "Dad made Sheridan a name anybody could trust, no matter whose side they were on. The fact that Pa Gillette did trust me ought to prove that. I've got to keep it that way, George. I've got to straighten this out."

Wolffe squeezed his arm, chuckling. "You couldn't get within a mile of the Gillettes now, anyway. Simmer down."

Sheridan nodded ruefully. "You're right. I was going to get some cash from the bank for a game."

"You'll only lose to Casket again. You dropped five hundred the last time."

"Don't start nagging at me about that again, George."

"But you're getting in too deep . . ."

"You've been saying that since you started handling the estate, and nothing's ever happened. Now drop it." Sheridan turned into the bank, thinking what a strange contrast they were to have become friends. George

165

Wolffe had been orphaned at twelve, had been forced to work as a stable hand to support his sister. At seventeen he had started studying law at night, and at twenty-one had passed the bar examination. He had gone into the office of Apache Wells' only other lawyer, and had soon become a full-fledged partner. The office handled all legal matters for the Double Bit, and, when Sheridan's father had died and Sheridan found out how little he had learned about running the big ranch, he had turned more and more to Wolffe for help. It had been a natural thing for Wolffe gradually to take over the management of all business matters concerning the vast Double Bit. It was a great relief for Sheridan to be left free to follow his gay and carefree life in town.

Although Wolffe was thinking in terms of thousands of cattle and hundreds of thousands of dollars now, the painful penny-pinching habits of his youth had never left him. It was a constant source of wonder to Sheridan that the man could be making such a handsome living himself now, could be dealing upon such a high financial plane, and still wear his threadbare clothes and begrudge the loss of a few hundred dollars at poker.

After leaving the bank, they walked back to the Black Jack. It was a long adobe-walled room with a bar on one side, a half dozen deal tables at the rear. The whole place smelled of damp sawdust and sweat and cheap whiskey and the homemade grape wine the Mexicans loved so much. There were three Double Bit hands at the bar, and Nacho, one of Sheriff Cline's deputies. He was a cat-eyed half-breed in rawhide *chivarras* that

166

clung to his legs like a second skin. He tilted his glazed sombrero back on his narrow head and shouted gaily at Sheridan.

"I buy you a drink for each time you punch Pa Gillette."

"How come it was you foreclosed on the Gillettes instead of the sheriff?" Sheridan asked.

"Sheriff Cline hear the Apache Kid was down near the county line." Nacho grinned. "I was the only one in the office to serve the eviction notice."

Sheridan shook his head. "I wish you hadn't done that."

Nacho laughed heartily. "Listen to him. Does that sound like the son of Tiger Sheridan? I myself saw Tiger turn a stampede once with nothing but a lighted match. It was a night like coal, and here they come, and he didn't have no horse or nothing . . ."

"You couldn't've seen him," one of the Double Bit hands said. "That happened before you was born."

"I don't even think it happened," the barman said, cleaning a glass. "It can't be done. Just one of those things you hear about Tiger Sheridan."

Nacho turned on the barman. "But it can be done, Jigger. The thing animals fear mos' is fire. Even a little flame like that."

Jigger put his tongue in one cheek and winked broadly at Sheridan, asking Nacho: "Would you like to try it?"

The deputy arched his chest, pounding on it. "Jus' give me the stampede. I show you."

167

"Let's go!" whooped one of the Double Bit hands. "I got just the cattle for you."

It was the old, good-natured ragging Sheridan had heard a hundred times, and he could not help feeling a return of his humor.

"All right," he said. "Joke's over. If Tiger was here, he'd throw you all out in the street for doubting that story."

Jigger put a bottle on the bar. "Heaven forbid. You know I don't any more doubt that story than I doubt me own existence."

Charlie Casket sat at one of the rear tables, his face gaunt and hollow-eyed in the dim light. "Pick a card, Brian."

Chuckling, Sheridan walked back to the table, taking a card from the pack Casket extended to him. He saw that it was a queen of hearts, then put it back without letting the gambler see its face. Casket let Sheridan shuffle and cut. Then Sheridan held the deck up for the gambler, and Casket picked out a card, turning its face to Sheridan.

"Queen of hearts," Wolffe said wonderingly.

"You're uncanny, Charlie," Sheridan said, sinking down into a chair. He held up a finger at the barman. "Bring the bottle, Jigger."

Ford Tarrant pushed through the door, saw Sheridan, and came back. Next to Sheridan, he was the biggest rancher in the section, a squarely framed, hearty man with a ruddy face and a quick and easy smile. With him was Jess Miller, who owned the Mercantile and several other businesses in town. He was plump

168

and prosperous in a rust-colored claw-hammer and expensive broadcloth pants, grunting expansively as he sat down between Tarrant and Casket.

"Heard you had a fight with Gillette," Tarrant said. "You must be convinced he's . . ."

"Forget it, Ford," Wolffe said sharply.

Tarrant looked up at Wolffe in surprise, then something fluttered through his eyes, and he chuckled. "Sorry, George."

Jigger brought over the bottle of Scotch from the case Sheridan always kept here, and poured the first round. Then they started the game. Sheridan won the first pot and raked it in, already on his second drink. It warmed him and relaxed him. This was another one of the good things in life, surrounded by friends, savoring their laughter, their jokes, their easy camaraderie.

Tarrant laughed, pulling a folded sheaf from his coat. "Now that Pa Gillette's out of the way, we ought to be able to push Mayor Prince's recall through."

Jess Miller poured Sheridan another drink, leaning forward confidingly. "You know how much weight your name bears in this country. Sign that petition and it'll draw the others like flies."

Sheridan let more whiskey slide down his throat, oil and fire in one. "I don't see why you want Prince out."

"Who do you think is pushing this franchise through for Arizona Mail and Freight?" Tarrant said. "Prince has enough influence over the council to get that franchise. With a railroad in Apache Wells, the Salt River bunch will be able to handle ten times the beef they do now."

169

Nacho wandered over, rolling a cigarette. "Is so, Sheridan. Only reason we've been able to keep the Salt Rivers from running bigger drives is that Tempe is so far away, and the Tarrant faction owns most of the water along the route."

"Mayor Prince is a Salt River man," Tarrant said. "You can't afford to let him get us over a barrel, Brian. Make this a shipping point, the Salt Rivers can handle more beef. The more beef they handle, the bigger they get. Let 'em get big enough and they'll squeeze us out. We've got to stop them before they begin. We've got proof that Prince was bribed by the railroad to push this franchise through, and we're going to recall him for it."

"What kind of proof?"

"Councilman Lewis overheard a division superintendent for Arizona Mail offer Prince a cut of the freight rates between here and Tempe . . ."

"Isn't that sort of flimsy evidence? Lewis has some dirt on his own coattails."

"It'll stand up in court if we don't let the Salt Rivers get any stronger," Tarrant said. "Now you promised me you'd sign the recall petition at the party the other night."

Sheridan took another long drink, squinting ruefully. "That party again."

Wolffe's voice was barely a murmur. "Now don't tell me you can't remember that, either?"

Sheridan looked at him for help. "Did I promise, George?"

"It was your word you were so worried about breaking a few minutes ago," Wolffe said.

Sheridan tried to focus his eyes. Wolffe seemed blurred. Miller poured him another drink. Sheridan chuckled affectionately at the cherubic little merchant.

"If I gave my word, I'll sign." Sheridan grinned. "I feel too good to hold up a game. Anybody got a pen?"

After that the game went on in earnest. Sheridan had no sense of time. It was the smoke-filled room and the soft laughter of men and the slap of cards and losing a pot or winning it and the cards becoming more and more blurred until he shoved his chair back, shaking his head and staring around the room. Wolffe was sitting at another table, a candle at his elbow, immersed in one of his law books.

"Anybody got the time?" Sheridan asked.

Tarrant yawned, looking at his watch. "Two o'clock."

"When a man's both drunk and tired, he'd better quit." Sheridan chuckled tipsily. "How much you owe me, Charlie?"

"You owe me," Casket said. "Eight hundred dollars."

CHAPTER
TWO

Ever since Sheridan's father had died, the old Double Bit house had been the scene of a party at least once a week. But now Brian had replaced the long, rambling adobe structure that Tiger Sheridan had built with a new house, a two-story frame with a steep gambrel roof and fancy dormers and all the ornate scrollwork and cupolas and gingerbread the Eastern architects had insisted was the rage now. The night after the poker game at the Black Jack, the poplars in front of the new Double Bit were lined with buggies and saddle horses, lights blazed from the windows, gay dance music reached out into the quiet night from the orchestra brought by special train from Tempe, and thence by stage to the ranch. There was a chef from Santa Fé to choose the imported liquors and oversee the making of the canapés and *hors d'oeuvres* the soft-footed Mexican servants were carrying through the crowd.

Sheridan stood near one of the French doors with Jess Miller and a couple of other friends from town. He made a handsome figure in his bottle-green frock coat and cream-colored trousers, the enjoyment of the scene flushing his face and bringing his hearty laugh.

172

"I never saw a man get such a kick out of life," the pudgy little merchant said.

Sheridan slapped Miller on the back. "As long as I've got my friends around me, I'm happy, Jess. What else is there?"

He felt his arm hooked by a soft, ringed hand, and looked around to see Arleen Wolffe smiling up at him.

"You've outdone yourself with the housewarming, Brian. It's such a wonderful service you do this town. They're all so hungry for a little bit of civilization. Do you like the orchestra?"

"Wonderful," he said. "I would have been lost without your help."

"Do you think they can spare you a couple of minutes?"

Grinning, Sheridan excused himself, allowing Arleen to pull him through an open French door to the gallery outside. She was as Indian-dark as her brother, black-haired, black-eyed, with something sensual to every movement of her slim body. Tonight she wore a clinging gown of shimmering gold satin that accentuated every lissome curve of her. A jeweled band around her shapely head pulled her dark brows into an exotic slant as she looked up at him. She moved her head close to his mouth, sniffing delicately.

"You've been drinking again."

He chuckled indulgently. "Man's got to have some vice."

"Like visiting Estelle Gillette?" she asked softly.

"I thought we weren't going to talk about that any more," he said. He bent to kiss her, pulling her body

173

hard against his, letting her satiny beauty flow through him like heady wine.

At last she pulled back. She was breathing more heavily, her eyes almost closed. But there was a pouting expression to her lips.

"You can't push it aside with kisses this time. You promised me you wouldn't see any more of Estelle."

"I guess I won't, now," he said ruefully. "Your brother foreclosed on the Gillettes yesterday. Estelle looked fit to claw my eyes out if I got within reach of her again."

She looked up at him with a strange calculation in her eyes. "Then you aren't going out there again?"

"I've got to see them," he said. "I've got to tell them George made a mistake. I can't foreclose on them."

She pulled away. "I don't believe you. That's just an excuse to see Estelle again."

"Don't be childish, Arleen. Even if I don't foreclose, it'll take them all a long time to get over this. They'll be suspicious for months. On the surface it looked like a dirty trick. I won't blame Estelle if she never speaks to me again."

"That proves you're really only thinking of her."

"How can you talk like this?"

"Because I don't like to share you." She brought the silken pressure of her body against him again. "What could you ever see in that little milksop, Brian? Peaches and cream and sweetness and light . . . and as shallow as Apache Creek in the summer. You need more of a woman than that. You've got depths and fires she could never touch."

174

"And you could?"

"Haven't I?"

This time it was she who kissed him. It was like a flame running through him and he realized how right she was. He had never known a woman with her boldness, her richness. Finally she pulled away, leaving him trembling faintly.

"Now. Promise me you won't go out there again."

He did not know whether it was the liquor or her exciting nearness making him so dizzy. But something kept prodding at him.

"Your brother didn't put you up to this?" he asked.

Her eyes widened. "Why would he have anything to do with it?"

"Tarrant wants Pa Gillette squeezed. George thinks it's for my own good. Some sort of political juggling."

"You know how I hate politics," she said impatiently. "I'm talking about Estelle, and nothing else. If you go out there again, I know it will be on account of her. If you go out there, Brian, I don't want to see you again."

Sheridan stared at her, his upper lip lengthening out into a long stubborn line. "I've got to go. I gave Pa my word."

He thought he saw surprise flutter through her eyes. It was blotted out by feline rage. Face white, she turned from him and went back inside. He started to follow, but a call from farther down the porch checked him.

He saw that it was his foreman. Latigo was a tall, heavily framed man in filthy blue jeans held up by a single snakeskin gallus. He never wore a shirt, but let

175

his red underwear suffice, the sleeves rolled up over the elbows of his gaunt forearms.

"I thought you'd want to see the tally books. We're bled white on three-year-olds, Mister Sheridan. We don't have a decent gather of anything to ship this year."

Sheridan shook his head impatiently. "Wolffe takes care of those things. You know that."

"I can't find him and I want to know what to do about that trail herd. Size it is, ain't no use making a drive . . ."

"Damn it, Latigo. Can't you see I'm busy? Come back tomorrow."

Sheridan tried to brush by him and go through the French doors, but Latigo caught his arm. "Look, Mister Sheridan, I rode all the way in here from the roundup just to . . ."

"Take your hands off me!"

For a moment longer Latigo held Sheridan, anger smoldering in his heavy-lidded eyes. Finally he let his hand slide off, the shadows seeming to deepen in the gaunt hollows beneath his blunt cheek bones.

"Someday, Mister Sheridan, you ain't going to talk that way with me and git away with it. You ain't going to talk that way at all."

Sheridan felt his whole body stiffen with rage. Then he realized what a fool he was being, and shook his head, passing a hand over his eyes.

"Sorry, Latigo. Everything seems wrong tonight. I've had too much to drink or something. I'll find Wolffe for you. He'll settle this."

176

There was no relenting in Latigo's dust-grimed, unshaven face. His eyes still smoldered with anger as Sheridan turned inside.

Brian found Wolffe, told him about the foreman, then went to the punch bowl for another drink. But that didn't remove his oppression. He had the sense of something wrong, out of joint, and yet he could not put his finger on it. Something more than Arleen or Latigo. Why did these things always seem to come up when he was drunk?

CHAPTER
THREE

A brazen sun beat down against the almost trackless floor of Skeleton Cañon until the heat waves rising from the parched sand formed a buttery haze in the rock-walled gorge. There was no sound except the small fretting *crackle* of wind through the baking creosote bushes. The sweat lay like oil on the shoulders of Brian Sheridan's steel-dust stallion and dripped steadily from beneath his hat brim to make greasy channels in the dust-caked mask of his face.

Sheridan was half sick from his hangover and still in a vile temper. He had started out this morning to tell the Gillettes they could stay on their property. He hadn't remembered it was such a grueling ride. He shook his head angrily, trying to dismiss the thought that he was being foolish.

By the very size of his holdings, he was automatically bound to the big ranchers who formed the Tarrant faction. The rift between the big and the small men inevitably placed him against the Gillettes. But their note went back to a time before any such rift had existed.

Tiger Sheridan had loaned Pa Gillette the money to start on. There had been friendship between the two families then, and it was upon this basis that Brian had promised Pa Gillette he would not press the note if Pa extended himself to buy more land. He had given his word, and his father had made the word of a Sheridan something that meant more in this lawless land than the bond of any bank. It was something Brian could not lose.

Suddenly his horse balked, whinnying sharply. He pulled it in, staring at its twitching ears, its wildly rolling eyes. He turned his squinted eyes up to the glittering rimrock of the cañon. Pa Gillette's words came to him: *There won't be a road safe for you to ride in all Arizona.*

He tried to down the tension in him and ride on. But when he reached a turn in the cañon, he pulled the horse up sharply, filled with a sudden insidious reluctance to go around it. Cursing himself, he put heels to the fiddling horse and forced it around the turn.

The sharp *crack* of the gunshot seemed to fill the cañon. He saw chips kicked out of a rock a foot to his right.

The horse reared up, pitching him off its rump. He hit heavily and flopped over on his belly. There were shooting pains through his right leg and that whole side of his body seemed numb. Desperately he crawled on his belly through the sand to the dubious protection of a boulder. He was sweating and trembling from shock.

Sprawled in the sand, he pulled his Bisley. He squinted his eyes against the sun, searching the rimrock. The strata of sandstone and shale up there gleamed crimson in the sunlight. He could see nothing. His horse was gone, out of sight and out of earshot. Then there was a glitter up on a ridge like sunlight on metal. He realized how exposed he was here. The glitter had come from across the cañon, and he had to cross to that side.

If they had not shot again that could mean they were getting into position. It gave him a small chance. His right leg was no longer numb although the pain was still there. He rose to his knees, throwing himself in a lunging run across the sandy floor. He dropped into the protection of a rock on the other side, surprised that there had been no shot. Then he began the climb to the rimrock.

It was a treacherous, exhausting struggle up to the top, squeezing through rocky fissures, scrambling laterally across the face of loose talus slopes. He reached a ledge halfway up and sank, exhausted, against a sun-baked rock. It seemed he could not get enough air. He was so dizzy from the exertion that he could not focus his eyes. Why should he be this played out? It hadn't been that hard a climb.

Still dizzy and panting, he pulled himself up for the rest of it. He reached the top so drained he had to sprawl on his belly behind the shelter of a lava uplift, unable to get to his feet. Finally he crawled to hands and knees, looking over the uplift to see that he was on an immense plateau that ran northward beyond sight. He crouched there until he saw a vague movement a few hundred yards down the rim of the cañon. He crawled on hands and knees out of the lava, using

180

jagged rocks and twisted junipers for cover. He was within fifty yards of the spot when a man suddenly appeared, working this way along the rim of the cañon. It happened so fast that Sheridan could not make out who it was.

All he saw was the dim form rising suddenly from behind a black clump of creosote, the glitter of sun on metal again. He jumped to his feet in his excitement, firing the first shot. His bullet kicked sand up in front of the man, obscuring him even more.

Sheridan ran thoughtlessly toward him, firing again and again. There was a shout and the man disappeared. Sheridan kept running until he reached the edge of a gully that ran back into the plateau from the rim of the cañon. He was going so fast he couldn't stop himself from running over onto the steep slope of the gully. He danced wildly to keep his feet as he slid down through the shale. He hit the bottom at a stumbling run with a vague impression of motion ahead of him where the gully made a turn. He fired again, twice, and then his hammer *clicked* on an empty chamber.

He brought himself up short, panting, dizzy again, realizing how foolish he had been, running in on the man this way. Like some fool kid with buck fever. Again he sought the cover of a jagged rock and crouched there on one knee, reloading his gun. His hands were shaking so badly he could hardly punch the shells from their chambers. Finally he got it reloaded and began to work his way down the cañon again. He reached the turn and moved around it with his gun cocked.

The gully pinched off here and he could see the prints of a horse in its sandy bottom. Sheridan halted, defeat dragging at his shoulders, as he realized the man was gone. Finally Sheridan turned and walked back through the gully till he reached the rim of Skeleton Cañon. His exhaustion forced him to admit how weak and soft these last years of rich living had left him and he wondered seriously if he had the strength to make it alive out of this desert on foot.

It was night when Sheridan reached the Double Bit, its gables and cupolas agleam in the moonlight. The feather-weight soles of his bench-made boots had been cut to ribbons hours ago by the sharp rocks of the desert; his feet were swollen and cut so badly that each step was an agony. His tattered clothes hung, slack and dust-filmed, on his stumbling body and he went to his knees once under the row of maple trees before finally gaining the porch.

His strange, stumbling figure startled the horses hitched at the cottonwood rack and they began whinnying and pulling at their reins. This must have been heard from inside for the door was swung wide. In the lamplight streaming out, Sheridan saw Arleen standing there, lustrous black hair framing the pale oval of her face.

"Brian!" she said sharply. Then she gathered up her full red skirt and came hurrying across the porch to keep him from falling.

He sagged gratefully against the soft warmth of her body. He felt her stiffen.

182

"George . . . ," she said. There was a strange brittle tone to her voice. "Come and get him."

George Wolffe and Ford Tarrant were already coming out the door. They caught Sheridan under the arms. He was vaguely aware of Arleen's stepping back, brushing the dust peevishly off her red dress.

"Somebody took a shot at me," Sheridan said as they helped him through the door. "My horse spooked and threw me."

Tarrant helped lower Sheridan to the sofa and then stepped back, taking his long black cigar out and thrusting his portly belly forward expansively. "If I was mayor, things like this wouldn't happen. That damned Prince is letting our town fill up with riff-raff . . ."

"Riff-raff hell," Wolffe said. "We all know who did this. There were a dozen people who heard the Gillettes threaten Brian yesterday."

Arleen poured a drink from the decanter on the desk. Sheridan took it and downed it neatly, seeing that Charlie Casket was in the living room, also. He sat in the big wing chair by the fireplace shuffling a pack of cards and had not offered to rise. He held the cards out, pokerfaced.

"Take one?"

Sheridan stared at him, too sick and beaten for clear thought. "What are you doing here, Charlie?"

"He thought you might like a little game tonight," Wolffe said. "Didn't know you'd gone out on that fool's errand to the Gillettes'. Are you convinced now that the foreclosure's got to stick?"

183

Sheridan settled back in the chair. "I can't quite believe they'd do anything as cold-blooded as that was."

"Don't be a fool!" Tarrant exploded harshly. "You've got to put Pa Gillette out of the game, Sheridan. The Salt River bunch will fall apart without him. And we can't be sure of Prince's recall unless he loses their support. The whole thing stands or falls on this Gillette deal."

Sheridan looked at Wolffe. "And you were the one who foreclosed on the Gillettes."

"Damn' it, Sheridan, it's for your own good," Wolffe said. "They try to kill you twice and you still can't see that. You're a big man. As long as that's true, men like Gillette and his crowd will be trying to pull you down. You've got to fight back."

Sheridan frowned at Tarrant. "You said if you were mayor. I thought you were putting Conners up against Prince on this recall petition."

Tarrant looked at his cigar. "Conners has backed down. I think the Salt River bunch reached him somehow."

"We nominated Tarrant at a special meeting today," Wolffe said. "Now, Brian, it's time you grew up and met your responsibilities. Give us your word you'll let that Gillette foreclosure stand. It's the only way we can protect ourselves."

Sheridan shook his head. "Not till I see the Gillettes."

"Brian's in no shape to talk politics," Arleen said soothingly. "Let me take him upstairs. You can talk this over tomorrow."

184

Sheridan looked up at her. "That won't do any good, either, Arleen."

She frowned at him. "What?"

"You made your bid last night at the party, and I still went out to see the Gillettes, didn't I? There isn't any use trying again."

Her face went white with rage. She cast a helpless glance at her brother. Something passed between them, and Arleen wheeled to leave the room. Sheridan could see that both her fists were clenched tightly.

"You force us to do this, Brian," Wolffe said. "Will you come into the study?"

Frowning in puzzled apprehension, Sheridan dragged himself from the chair and followed Wolffe down the hall, with Casket and Tarrant behind. The study door was open.

Latigo sat with one leg on the desk, a pile of tally books beside him. He was still in his dust-grayed jeans and red underwear, and his eyes met Sheridan's insolently.

"We might as well start with Casket," Wolffe said.

The gambler pulled a sheaf of papers from his pocket. "They're checks and I.O.U.s, Brian," he said. "You'd be surprised how much you've lost to me in those card games over the last couple of years. It amounts to around thirty thousand dollars."

Sheridan felt hot anger well up in him at the implications. "You mean you've been saving those things . . . ?" He broke off, staring at Tarrant. "You have a motley collection on your payroll, Ford. We'll go to the bank tomorrow. I'll get the cash."

"Your personal account is overdrawn," Wolffe said. "I got the bank statement today."

"Then we'll get it from the business account."

"That well's dry, too," Wolffe said, tapping a pile of papers on the desk. "With no money in your personal account, I had to put these through the business account. They're the bills for the house. It cost you over fifty thousand dollars, and only part of it's paid for."

Sheridan wheeled to him. "There was more than that in the business account the last time I went over the books with you."

Wolffe shook his head. "You forget the parties. Last night cost over four thousand dollars. You've thrown a dozen of them this year already."

"Damn you . . ." Sheridan started to say they'd sell some stock. Then he sensed what Latigo was here for, and stared down at the beef books.

"I tried to tell you last night." Latigo said. "We've still got a big herd, but its all too young to ship for beef. You bled us white on three-year-olds to pay for that trip East last year."

"Then we'll sell the stuff right here," Sheridan said, desperation entering his voice. "Every man in Gila County would give his right arm for some Double Bit cattle."

"And pay you with a note," Tarrant said sarcastically. "Nobody has that kind of cash around here."

Sheridan looked helplessly at Wolffe, who shook his head. "You've gotten yourself into this hole, Sheridan."

"And you let me. You knew what they were up to!"

Wolffe flushed. "How many times did I try to stop you from having these parties, Brian, from gambling, from wasting your money on whims?"

"If Charlie presses these gambling debts, it'll ruin you," Tarrant said. "He'd have to slap an attachment on your property to get the money and it'd be around town in five minutes. You'd have a hundred creditors up here pounding on your door. Hadley'd foreclose his mortgage on this house and those Eastern architects would attach your stock for what you still owe them. You wouldn't have the shirt left on your back."

Sheridan stared around the circle of their faces, physically sick with the realization of how they had used him.

"All you have to do is give us your word you'll let the Gillette foreclosure stand," Tarrant said. "And Charlie won't press these gambling debts."

Sheridan realized he was trembling with his anger. "Get out," he said. "This is still my house. As long as I own it, nobody who'd pull a deal like that is going to stay in it."

"They didn't want to do it this way, Brian," Wolffe said. "You made them. It's for your own good, don't you realize that . . . ?"

Sheridan had not reacted to anger this violently in a long time. Face white with rage, he yanked open the desk drawer and whipped out the old Colt dragoon his father had always kept there.

"If the whole bunch of you snakes isn't out of here in one minute, this is going off in somebody's face!"

CHAPTER
FOUR

There was nothing much Sheridan could do that night. He was too sick and too filled with frustrated rage to sleep. He spent half the time pacing his room in his bathrobe, trying to figure a way out of this. At five he had the cook fix him black coffee and toast and half an hour later he was in the saddle on the way to the Gillettes. This time he wore his Bisley and had a Winchester in the saddle boot. He did not take the Skeleton Cañon route but rode through the badlands north of the cañon.

It was mid-morning and already burning hot by the time he reached the Gillettes', beaten down by the ride. They had a little greasy-sack outfit in the foot slopes of the Apaches. He passed through a poor man's gate, with Sheriff Cline's notice tacked on one of the cottonwood poles, and rode warily in toward the adobe house and corrals. There was no stock in the corrals, however, and a strange quiet hung over everything. He rode up to the door, saw that it was ajar. He stepped down, went inside. The house was empty. The Gillettes had already left.

He went wearily back to his horse, seeing how it was closing about him. The Salt River bunch was strung out

188

along the river for many miles toward Tempe, and the next man down was Wirt Peters. He had once worked for Tarrant, but had struck out on his own, and had subsequently become a great friend of the Gillettes. Sheridan headed for his place, reaching it in the heat of midday, hoping Peters was not out on roundup.

The man was a bachelor, with a little two-room adobe set back in a gash between two ridges. He apparently had been out on nearby roundup, for his horse and the animals of his two Mexican hands stood, channeled with sweat, by the ramada under which the three men were eating.

Peters rose as Sheridan rode in. He was a big man, the heat giving his flesh a ruddy glow through the scrubby blond beard making a stubble of his jaw. His blue shirt was plastered to his beefy muscles with sweat, and brush scars made illegible etchings in the film of dust graying his batwing chaps.

Sheridan drew rein before him, leaning out of the saddle. "Wirt, you seen the Gillettes?"

"I have not," Peters said.

"Cline evicted them," Sheridan said. "I've got to find them."

Raw anger exploded in Peters's voice. "What the hell you coming to me for? I ought to gun you off the place. Maybe you think you can foreclose on me, too."

"I didn't even want to foreclose on them, Wirt. There's been a mistake. It goes for you, too. For everybody I hold a note on. I could call those notes in if I wanted. But the name of Sheridan would never mean anything again in this land. I gave my word to Pa

I wouldn't call in his note even if it went overdue. It's the same to you. Only I need your help. Can you give me any cash at all on what you owe? I'm in a hole, Peters."

The man studied his horse, spat into the dust. "You must be in a hole to beat yourself down thataway. I never seen you exert yourself beyond reaching for a drink in all your life. I can't give you any cash, Brian. This land don't leave a man anything."

Sheridan felt himself sink against the saddle. "How about Purdy?"

"His wife's had another baby. He didn't even have the money for the doctor."

Sheridan took a ragged breath. "All right. At least pass the word along to the Gillettes."

"I'll do that." The wind-wrinkles fanned out from Peters's quizzical eyes as he gazed up at Sheridan, his voice half-mocking, half-sympathetic. "I always thought life was going to turn around and kick you in the teeth one of these days, Brian."

Sheridan rode the day out seeking the Gillettes and looking up the men who owed the Double Bit money. But everywhere it was the same story. He stayed that night with one of the Mexican families who had served his father in the early days, filled with the sick realization that he could not get any help out here.

He hit Apache Wells the next day, dust-grayed and beaten out by the constant riding, and went first to Jess Miller's Mercantile. The store was a single big room in a frame building filled with the linty smell of fresh calico and the sick-sweet odor of black-strap sorghum.

Miller sat on a high stool back in the gloom, a pencil over his ear, his body humped over a ledger. Somehow he didn't look as cherubic or expansive as he had seemed at their poker games. There was a pinched look to his face as he worked on the figures. Then he heard Sheridan's footfall and looked up sharply.

"Jess," Sheridan said. "You and I've been friends a long time . . ."

Miller took the pencil cautiously from his ear. "Yes, Brian?"

"I'll say it straight. I need a loan. I saw you through those first two rough years and I thought you might be willing to return the favor."

"I've only got a couple of hundred in the safe, Brian. That be enough?"

"It's got to be fifty or sixty thousand, Jess."

The man's eyes popped open. "Lord, Brian, you won't find that much money in all Apache Wells."

Sheridan leaned toward him. "I know what kind of money you've been pulling in, Jess, and I know you've got the cash. I'm asking you as a friend . . ."

"I can't do it, Brian." Something furtive went through the man's pale eyes. "You're wrong about my money. It's been a bad year for everybody. A man has to hang onto what little money he's got."

Sheridan straightened slowly. "You do that," he said at last in a disgusted voice. "You just do that."

He walked out of the store at a savage stalk, halting on the sidewalk outside. But defeat was draining the anger from him. Miller had been his last bet. He knew to go to Troy Hadley would be useless. The banker was too shrewd a businessman to put money in a losing proposition. And it was a losing proposition. More and more Brian saw that.

The planks began to tremble and he turned to see Jim Murphy coming toward him. Murphy was a paunchy, middle-aged lawyer from Tempe. He cleared his throat uncomfortably as he halted before Sheridan.

"Glad I found you, Brian. Just got in on the stage. Going up to your place. Glad I found you."

Sheridan tried to regain some of his old jauntiness. "What for, Jim? Trying to cut Wolffe out of some business?"

"Not that, son . . ." Murphy loosened his collar, looking out into the street. "Truth of the matter is some bills you owe were put before the court at Tempe. They got in touch with Wolffe and found out you can't meet payment. Truth of the matter is, I've been appointed receiver by the court."

"Receiver? I haven't declared bankruptcy yet."

"Wolffe did that for you. He has your power of attorney. Uh . . . we'll give you time to vacate the premises, of course. House goes up for auction the eighth."

Sheridan felt all the blood drain from his face. "They sure as hell didn't waste any time, did they?"

"Wolffe has the papers in his office, if you want to sign 'em." Murphy pulled at his sweat-drenched collar. "I don't like this any more'n you do, Brian."

Brian felt his shoulders sag. "I suppose not."

He turned heavily and walked down toward Wolffe's office. It was a small office over the feed store, reached by a rickety outside stairway. Wolffe sat before a big battered desk in the front room, writing something, and glanced up sharply as Sheridan entered. The dust-filmed windows washed out the strong sunlight till it lit Wolffe's face with a sallow tint, settling deep shadows in the strongly marked grooves and hollows of his heavy-boned face.

"It's like you to run out on your responsibilities," he said acidly. "I've looked high and low for you, Brian. They've got us backed against the wall."

"I should be mad as hell with you, George," Sheridan said. "But somehow I can't."

Wolffe leaned forward, fixing the disturbing intensity of his burning eyes on Sheridan's face. "How often did I try to stop that profligate spending of yours? It was you that got us into this hole. When I saw what Tarrant planned, what could I do? You can still save yourself if you'll play along with Tarrant. He can have Casket's suit withdrawn. He might even get Troy Hadley to loan you the money to take care of the other creditors that have started clamoring."

"All I have to do is go back on my word to Gillette," Sheridan said thinly.

"You can't look at it that way . . ."

"I do." Sheridan stared out the dusty window. "It's funny. I guess I've asked help from every friend I had. It's funny how different they look when you need help. I'm dead busted, George."

"You will be if you don't use your head."

"It makes a man think. I guess it's the first time I've really thought in all my life. When all your money's gone, when every friend you had runs out on you . . . all you have left is your word . . ."

"Brian . . ."

"That's all I have left of what Dad built here, Wolffe. But it's the greatest thing of them all. I'm not going to lose it, too." He wheeled toward the man. "Murphy said you had some papers to sign. I suppose I might as well get it over with."

After he left Wolffe's, he seemed too drained to feel anger any more. Or defeat. Or anything. It seemed as if these last two days had used up his capacity for emotion. He was filled with a great apathy. He supposed part of it was a physical let-down after the endless hours of riding. Force of habit made him seek relief in a drink. His steel-dust was still hitched in front of the Mercantile, halfway between Wolffe's office and the Black Jack. As he turned to go to the saloon, he saw a man at the hitch rack, untying the reins.

Sheridan started toward him at a hard walk. "That's my horse, Latigo."

"Not any more," the foreman said. "The receivers are up at your house, checking all the stock. This horse was missing."

Sheridan reached him, yanking the reins out of his callused hands. "It's my personal animal. They can't take a man's horse any more than they can take his pants."

Latigo's eyes grew heavy-lidded with insolence. "They gave me my orders. They won't be able to pay off all your debts with what they got. This horse is worth twenty-five hundred dollars. I'll take the reins."

"The hell you will!" Sheridan threw the rawhide lines over the stallion's head and swung around to toe the stirrup.

Latigo caught his shoulder and swung him back. Sheridan's foot was hung up in the stirrup and he knew he was going to fall anyway, so he let his momentum pitch his body around into Latigo. It knocked the man back against the hitch rack. The hip-high bar flipped Latigo helplessly backward onto the sidewalk. And Sheridan went on his face in the dirt, his foot still caught in the stirrup.

The excited stallion reared up. Sheridan felt his boot tear free. At the same time, Latigo rolled over and gained his feet. His eyes were almost shut with rage. As Sheridan tried to rise, the foreman jumped right back over the rack at him.

Sheridan could not roll aside soon enough. He heard his own shout of pain as Latigo's spiked heels stabbed into his back and drove him down into the dirt. Latigo jumped off Sheridan and swung a kick at his face.

It made a bright explosion of pain in Sheridan's consciousness. He rolled away, hugging his arms around his head. He had a dim view of Latigo's legs churning toward him and knew another kick would finish him. He came to his knees and launched himself bodily at hip height.

He threw his weight into Latigo and clamped his arms around the man, driving him backward. The man tripped on the curb and went down. Sheridan sprawled

195

across him, dimly aware of men spilling out of the Black Jack, of a crowd gathering.

Sheridan tried to slam a blow at Latigo. The man blocked it and pitched him off. Sheridan rolled away, trying to gain his feet. He was reaching for air like a windsucker. When he got his feet under him, his legs wobbled like a newborn calf's. How could he be so weak?

He saw Latigo come up and lunge for him. He staggered backward, trying to set himself. The man shifted around before him and threw a blow. Sheridan put up an arm to block it and came in under, slashing at Latigo's belly. He heard Latigo grunt. But it did not knock the foreman backward. The man swept Sheridan's guard aside, laughing hoarsely.

"That high living sure left you like jelly."

The blow came on the last words. It knocked all the wind from Sheridan. He felt himself stagger backward, a retching sound torn from him. He saw Latigo come into him again and tried to wheel away. He felt Latigo's hands cup over the back of his neck, jerking him down. Then Latigo's knee smashed into his face.

He seemed to spin away in a blinding spasm of pain. He was on the ground. He heard somebody breathing heavily out in front of him and started crawling toward the sound.

"The fool don't know when to quit," somebody in the crowd said. "Kick him again, Latigo. Tear the other ear off . . ."

The world came down and smashed him on the side of the head and he was spinning again and there was

196

pain and the vague sounds all around him and somebody laughing. It took him a long time to realize he was lying on his face against the curb. He tried to lift his head but he couldn't see anything. He made an effort to rise, but could not. He rolled over on his side, pawing blood and dirt from his eyes.

Finally dim vision returned. Knots of men were still clustered along the sidewalk, watching him. He recognized Nacho, with an evil leer on his face, and Jigger, still holding a bar towel. Jess Miller had come out of his Mercantile, but made no move to cross the street. Latigo was up on the prancing stallion. From this triumphant height, he sent one last look down at Sheridan, and spat. Then he raked the steel-dust into a dead run down the street toward his own horse hitched at another rack.

A woman in a blue dress pushed her way through the loose group of men, stepping off the curb. More a girl than a woman. A girl with honey hair swirled around her shoulders by the breeze. He felt a deep humiliation stain his cheeks. She dropped to her knees beside him, seeking his handkerchief in his coat, dabbing at his face with it.

"I shouldn't feel sorry for you," Estelle Gillette said. "But I can't help it." She helped him sit up. "We heard talk. Does this mean it's true?"

He nodded sickly. "I'm wiped out." He shook his head ruefully. "I guess I don't even have a horse now."

"How could they do it? The Double Bit was the biggest thing in this country."

197

"Tarrant set it up. As long as I was with him, the Salt Rivers couldn't pull his bunch down. The Sheridan name meant too much in this country. But Tarrant must've known the day would come when I'd see how they were using me. As blind as I was to the things going on here, it wouldn't last forever. He maneuvered things till my back was against the wall. When I finally balked, he put the pressure on. I guess he thought I'd knuckle under to save the Double Bit."

"And you didn't?" A strange new light began to shine in her eyes. Then she shook her head in a puzzled way. "But what about George Wolffe? Surely he knew what was going on."

"I guess I can't really blame George. He was always trying to make me take more interest in the politics of Apache Wells. He tried his best to keep me from living so high. I guess he was really looking out for my best interests. And when he saw it was too late, I guess he played along with Tarrant to try and pull me out of the hole."

"Where will you go now?"

He shook his head. "I don't know. I'll have to get a job, I guess."

"What kind of job? You never took enough of an interest in cattle to know anything about them. You can't keep books. You're too soft for any job that calls for hard labor. All you ever did was drink and gamble and have parties."

He stared dully at the street. "I guess you're right. I couldn't get a job anywhere."

"Especially not in this town. The Salt River bunch hates you too much and the other side wouldn't help you for fear of a kick back from Tarrant. So you'll starve to death. Or join the barflies in the Black Jack cadging drinks and scavenging in the garbage pails out back."

He winced under the merciless light of her words. It was an incredible picture she painted, but he realized how close to the truth it was.

"We're staying at Chino Sandoval's," she said. "Why don't you come out there?"

He looked up at her. "That's crazy. The only people in Apache Wells who offer me help are the ones who have the most cause to hate me."

The soft shape of her mouth hardened. "You'd better take the offer. It's the only place you can go."

CHAPTER
FIVE

Chino Sandoval had a one-horse outfit up by Mescal Springs, high in the Apaches. It was a land rutted and scarred by the fires of Nature till there was little left but bleak buttes and mesas and the eastern backbone of the mountains etching a purple outline against a sun-bleached sky. The springs were but a sink hollowed out of the rocks, dry as bone during the summer days, turned to viscid mud by the water that rose to the surface when night came.

It was a fifteen-mile drive from Apache Wells, and Sheridan was sore and beaten by the ride as well as the fight long before they reached the cut-off that wound up onto the mesa commanding the springs. Here, in the feeble shade of scrawny cottonwoods, were the adobe buildings, the ratty fences of ocotillo corrals.

A dozen children scampered out of the compound like scared chickens, hiding behind mud walls and in dark doorways, peering owlishly at the wagon as it pulled up before the house. Then the men began to drift in from the corrals. Pa Gillette and Asa were first in sight, stalking toward the wagon. Surprised anger dug great hollows in Pa's gaunt cheeks.

200

"What call you got to bring that snake up here, Estelle?"

"It's the only place he could come," Estelle said defiantly. "They've pulled everything out from under him. The Double Bit's wiped out. It's even worse than when we lost everything. He doesn't even know how to work. He can't get a job in town. All his friends turned on him. We've got to give him a chance, Pa."

"Like the chance he give us?" Pa said. Asa wheeled off toward the house, and Pa glanced after him. "Asa, where you going?"

"To get my gun," Asa said.

"You stay out here!" Sandoval called, coming up from behind them. "You promise no trouble there be."

Asa paused reluctantly, looking back at him. Sandoval was a small, wiry man with all the fat melted off his bones by the sun and incredible hardships of this arid country. His eyes were startlingly blue in an almost Negroid face. One of the dozen children peering around the corner of the house had blond hair. It lent a dubious credence to Sandoval's claim that he was pure Yaqui Mayo, descended from the shipwrecked Norsemen who were supposed to have landed at the mouth of the Mayo River hundreds of years before the Spaniards came.

Estelle jumped down to the ground, her voice intense. "You've got Brian wrong, Pa. He didn't order anybody to foreclose on us. Just two days after the fight in town, he came out to tell us we didn't have to move, and we shot at him."

"Shot at him!" Pa said.

201

"Maybe you didn't know about it," Sheridan said, looking at Asa. "It was up at Skeleton Cañon."

"Asa was with me all that day," Pa stormed. "We was moving down here. Chino can vouch for that."

"*Es verdad*," the Yaqui said. "It's the truth."

A pair of Mexican hands had moved up behind Sandoval, and Cameron was coming heavily in after them. Sheridan looked around the circle of their hostile faces.

"Somebody bushwhacked me in the cañon," he said. "If it hadn't been for that, I'd have been out to tell you to stay on your land."

"It was all some deal of Tarrant's," Estelle said. "He knew the Salt River bunch would be lost without you, Pa. The very fact that they've ruined Brian should be proof enough of where he stands."

The anger still moved turgidly through Pa's face, and Asa spat disgustedly. "It's some trick. I say fill him full of buckshot if he ain't off here in two minutes."

"Why should man his size stoop to trick?" Sandoval asked. "I knew his father. The Sheridans are no like that."

Estelle turned toward the Yaqui. "You helped us when we needed it, Chino. Now help him. He needs it worse than we did."

From the pouch every Mexican carried at his belt Sandoval pulled a bundle of *hojas*. He fingered one of these pieces of Indian cornhusk free, tapping into it a small quantity of tobacco from a small tube also contained in the pouch.

202

"I never thought I see the day a Sheridan to me would come for help," he murmured. He put the *hojas* back into the pouch, rolling the cigarette. "Can cattle you work?"

"He'll learn," Estelle said.

From the pouch, Sandoval now pulled flint and steel and a red cord of tinder. He struck spark from the flint with the steel *eslabón,* and it lodged in the tinder. He blew it into flame and lit his cigarette.

"At his hands look. Like lilies. Can a man so soft learn about work in one lifetime?"

"Just give him a chance," Estelle pleaded.

"You'll have to work like hell. Everybody out here they have to work like hell. The land she's like that."

"I'll try to pay for my keep, Chino."

Sandoval grinned suddenly. "Then w'at you sit there for? Juan, Pancho, get grub from wagon the little girl she bring."

Sheridan got stiffly out of the wagon. Over the sweaty rumps of the team, he saw Pa still staring at him. There was truculent hatred in the man's eyes, and Sheridan realized this was far from settled.

Sheridan slept that night in a bear-grass hut down by the river with the Gillettes and the two Mexicans. He got little sleep, tossing restlessly on the hard corn-shuck pallet, listening to the rasping snores of the tall, thin hand called Juan. It was still dark when Sandoval came in and shook him by the shoulder.

"Drags your navel, you lazy *cucarachas.* Is time to roll out if we be at Cañon Moro by sunup."

They rolled out cursing and grumbling. Estelle was with the women up by the house, serving coffee and beef and beans. Still sore and stiff from his beating, Sheridan almost gagged on the greasy food. With a *clatter* of tinware the men tossed empty plates and cups into the wreck pan and drifted toward the corrals. When Sheridan reached the corral, Pancho came over with a rawhide jumper and a pair of Mexican *chaparejos* slung over one arm.

"Here's clothes, *señor*. Better get extra pair pants from somebody, too. Those thorns out on the *malpais* they stab like the dirk. Chino he tell me to help with your horses. That one with the *lobo* stripe down his back has lots of bottom."

Sheridan struggled into the jumper and chaps. The man thrust a maguey rope into his hands and they moved into the mill of animals lifting a curtain of dust over the corral. Juan and Sandoval and the three Gillettes were all roping their animals out, shouting and cursing. Sheridan got kicked down trying to dab an awkward loop on the *lobo*-striped dun. Pancho finally heeled the animal and put a blind on him while he was down. Then he got a Mexican-tree saddle off the top bar of the corral and slung it on. With fumbling hands, Sheridan cinched it up. He was drenched with sweat and caked with dust by the time he was through.

Pancho helped him rope out two more horses for his string. Then Sheridan stepped aboard his dun. It started pitching before he got his right leg swung over the saddle, and he went off like an empty sack. He heard Asa laugh derisively from somewhere in the dust. Sandoval came riding up on a nervous buckskin.

"These horse got little more vinegar than ones you're used to, no, *amigo?*"

Sheridan tried again and this time stayed on. After the bronco got rid of its morning orneriness, cat-backing around the corral, it settled down. And they rode.

He had no measure of time. Or of the distance they covered. When it was light enough to see, they had reached a spot where a half dozen brush-filled cañons opened out into a sink with a cow trail leading down every wash to the water. Sandoval said they would round up the cattle while they were drinking and run them down to the flats where they'd have swing room for their ropes.

The men sat sourly in their saddles, half asleep. With the first touch of sun the cattle came, spooky, wild creatures, testing the air with their lifted snouts, shambling down to the water. Sheridan peered through the milky dawn at their gaunt silhouettes.

"How can you make any money off that beef?" he whispered.

"We don't," Sandoval said. "That's why small we remain while big you get. Cattle don't put on any lard in the badlands. But jack rabbits they won't take in Tempe, *amigo*. We do the best we can."

Juan came threading in through a coulée from the higher land, whispering hoarsely: "That is all, *señores*. We can jump them now."

With a whoop, they rushed down on the herd. The cattle jumped like scared jacks and headed at a dead run down the cañon. The nimble-footed horse took Sheridan in a wild, scrambling run down the steep pitch of the cañon as they drove the frenzied cattle into the flats. The Gillettes were waiting by the branding fires and they surrounded the cattle and put them into a mill. While they held them, the cutting and branding began.

"Cut me out that brindle with the gotch horn!" Pa shouted at Sheridan.

Sheridan put his bronco into the herd. A cow took a swipe at him and he almost got gored. He wheeled his bronco and got pinched between two milling heifers. He tore one leg off his chaps getting out of that, and, by the time he pulled free, the brindle was out of sight.

"Cut me out a dogie, if you can't do any better than that!" Pa roared. "That pied one right in front of you."

Sheridan saw the motherless calf ahead of him and touched his excited horse with a heel. The animal drove in behind the dogie, forcing it out into the open. The little calf tried to wheel back at the fringe of the herd and Sheridan cut in between it and the other cows, turning it back. The air was so thick with dust he could no longer see Pa, but he pushed the dogie hard toward the spot the man had been in.

Too late, he saw the rope ahead of him. It was stretched taut from Asa's buckskin to a downed steer. Asa had dallied his end of the line around the saddle horn and was just swinging off. The dogie hit the stretched rope first, tripping on it and going down.

206

Sheridan saw Asa's horse jerk. One foot out of the stirrup, Asa threw himself back in the saddle to keep from being pitched. Sheridan tried to wheel his horse away but he was going too fast. He ran into the line a second after the dogie hit.

This jerked Asa's horse so heavily it almost lost its footing. Dancing to remain erect, it spun around into Sheridan's animal as he wheeled to the right. He saw the dallied rope pull free and fall to the ground. The steer scrambled to its feet, and disappeared in the dust, line trailing.

Asa's horse tried to dance away from Sheridan's line. Asa reined it back in till he was knee to knee with Sheridan, grabbing at his jumper.

"Damn you!" he shouted. "You did that on purpose!"

Sheridan tried to tear free but Asa hung on. A sudden shift of their excited horses unbalanced Sheridan and he pitched into Asa, carrying him out of the saddle. They hit heavily. Sheridan rolled groggily away from Asa. The wiry Gillette gained his feet first and jumped Sheridan, lashing one boot out to rowel Sheridan's face with the spur.

There was the smashing detonation of a shot. Sheridan heard the whining ricochet of metal on metal. He stared, wide-eyed, at the boot lifted above his face, seeing that the rowel was gone from the spur.

"You better put it down on the ground, Asa," Sandoval said. "Next time your foot I shoot off."

Asa let his boot drop back to the ground beside Sheridan's face. Sheridan rolled over onto hands and knees. Sandoval was sitting a dancing horse right above them, a smoking Colt in his hand.

"Now back to work get, both of you," he said. "Any more of this and the welcome of my house she's no longer yours."

For two weeks the roundup continued. Days that never seemed to end. Up before dawn and in the saddle till long after dark. Sleeping in stupefied exhaustion through a night too short to give a man any real rest. The wink of branding fires in the velvet dark. The constant stench of sweat and burning hair and hot dust.

It was a nightmare for Sheridan. He lost weight till his clothes hung on him and his face was raw from the burn of sun and wind and his whole body ached with the slightest movement.

A hundred times he was ready to quit. It was hard to say why he stayed. Sometimes it was Asa's goading, making him stick in sheer bitter defiance. Sometimes it was the shy friendship of Sandoval, filling him with a warmth he had never felt with Jess Miller or the other men he had thought were close to him. Sometimes it was his own stubbornness, a stubbornness he had never known he possessed before, lengthening that long upper lip into a fighting shape and putting him back into the nightmare.

After the branding was over, they cut out the young stuff and started the beef toward Tempe. They had long since used up the coffee and beans Estelle had gotten at Apache Wells, and were living exclusively on their own beef. But they had no time to stop off at the ranch.

Sandoval had started roundup early in the hope of beating the big operators into Tempe, and it would be touch and go from now on.

They drove west out of the Apaches and into the alkali furnace of the flats south of the Superstitions. At this time of year there was so little water that they worked on a dangerously close margin between sinks. They reached Denver Wells and found it dry. They pushed a herd frantic with thirst on toward Rabbit Sink, the next water hole, the men as hollow-eyed and driven as the animals.

They topped a sandhill east of the sink near nightfall, and saw that the cattle had run up against something ahead. In the haze of wind-blown sand, all Sheridan could see was the dim forms of the beasts milling back and forth in the flats, as if held by an invisible wall.

Sandoval and Sheridan put their jaded horses to a trot, rounding the herd and catching sight of Asa and Pa Gillette ahead. Then Sheridan saw the triple strand of barbwire.

"This sink belongs to Sid Bouley, don't it?" Asa said acidly. "I thought he was still with the Salt River bunch."

Sandoval's coffee-colored brow knotted as he stared at the fence. "Bouley always a weak bet was. Look like he went over to Tarrant when he heard Pa was squeeze' out."

"We'll cut the wire, damn it," Pa said. "Juan, bring up that hatchet. These cattle will die if they don't get this water."

The thin Mexican galloped up, pulling a hatchet from his bedroll. The cattle were frenzied with their thirst, milling against the fence in a bawling press. Sandoval told Asa to hold the beef there till he found out if there was any water. Sheridan and Pa went with him through the hole Juan chopped.

Some 300 yards on they came to the sloping banks of the sink. In the dusk, Sandoval was a vague shadow, dismounting.

"Is mud. The water in an hour should surface." He turned to call: "Start them through!"

It was getting so dark Sheridan could not see the cattle at first. He knew they were beginning to move, for their bawling grew in a raucous crescendo. Then the ground began to tremble and the first tossing heads appeared out of the gloom. Sandoval toed his stirrup and started to swing up.

Then the gunshot came, like the crack of a giant whip. Sheridan's startled horse screamed in fright and reared high. He put a rein against its neck and spurred a sweaty flank, bringing the animal back down and spinning it to keep the beast from bolting.

More shots formed a *crackling* drumbeat in the night. Sheridan fought his spinning horse, staring into the darkness in a vain attempt to see where they came from. Sandoval's horse had bolted while he was still only half on and he was racing away from the sink, striving to gain the saddle.

"It's coming from those north ridges!" Pa shouted. "The cattle's stampeding . . ."

His voice broke off sharply, amid the drumming bursts of gunfire, and Sheridan saw him pitch from his saddle. The ground was shaking with the rush of cattle now and Sheridan knew he had but a moment to reach the man. He spurred the frightened line-back horse across the sandy flats, pulling it down hard where Pa's gaunt form stirred feebly on the ground.

"Grab a stirrup, Pa!" he shouted. "I'll have to drag you out!"

The man made a feeble attempt to lift his arm, dropped back. Sheridan swung down and tried to hold his frenzied horse and catch Pa under the armpits. As he heaved the man up, meaning to throw him over the saddle, more shots split the night. The horse reared, snapping the reins from Sheridan's hand, and bolted. He was left holding Pa halfway off the ground, without a horse.

The tossing heads and curving horns of the cattle seemed to be right on top of them. Sheridan had a dim glimpse of a rider off to one side, and heard Juan's high voice.

"Run to the left, Sheridan! I can't turn them! You can make it to the left!"

He let Pa's limp weight slide to the ground, his whole body jerking with the impulse to wheel and race for safety. But something held him. A thought from long ago was in his mind. And Jigger's words. *It can't be done. It's just one of those stories you hear about Tiger Sheridan.*

Even as it ran through him, Sheridan was reaching for the match in a hip pocket and wiping it against his

211

Levi's. It didn't catch. The ground was quaking beneath him and it seemed another instant would bring the whole herd down on him. He struck the match again.

It flared, wavered. He cupped it in his hand. He held it that way, standing, spraddle-legged, over Pa Gillette's body, his whole being torn by the primitive impulse to escape the destruction of those tossing horns and cloven hoofs bearing down on him.

For that last moment he stared up at the oncoming phalanxes, and thought he was through. Jigger was right. It couldn't be done.

Then the steer right before him reared into the air, eyes rolling wildly in animal fear of fire. The next animal veered the other way, bawling in senseless fright at that small, winking flame.

The others followed suit blindly, splitting around Sheridan. He was an island in a sea of sweaty bodies and tossing horns. The light flickered, seemed to die. He saw a heifer racing right at him. Desperately he cupped his hands about the match. The flame flared again. The heifer threw her head back to bawl and almost lost her feet turning aside in the last instant.

If it had been a Double Bit gather, he would never have lasted it out. But the very meagerness of Sandoval's outfit saved him. It seemed an eternity. It seemed a second. Then they were gone, leaving him still standing above Pa, unable to tell whether the earth was still trembling beneath him, or whether he was shaking in reaction. The match burned his fingers and he threw it from him. Its light winked out and left the blackness of night.

212

CHAPTER
SIX

It was near evening of the next day that they got back to Sandoval's ranch, Asa and Cameron riding with Pa between them, and Sheridan bringing up the rear. They couldn't have gotten a wagon out to the Rabbit Sink country, so they had been forced to bring Pa back on his horse. It had been a cruel ride for him, and he was half delirious in the saddle.

Estelle was the first to come from the house, staring blankly at the little group of alkali-covered riders, then breaking forward with a sharp cry. Sheridan dismounted and helped Cameron ease the elder Gillette out of his saddle. He opened fever-rimmed eyes as Estelle reached him, suppressed hysteria in her pale face.

"It's all right, Daughter," he said feebly. "Little gunshot wound ain't going to hurt me after what we went through. Brian saved my life. He's a real Sheridan, all right. Nobody'd ever believe that story about his pa. He proved it. Just a match like that. Just a little match . . ." He winced and sagged forward against Sheridan.

With a small sob, Estelle turned and helped them half carry him toward the house. It was then that

Sheridan noticed the two dusty horses at the door, and the pair of men who had followed Estelle.

Morton Forge was a thick-thewed man in a linsey-woolsey coat and brush-scarred leggings of rawhide, the ruddy hue of a perpetually sunburned face glowing faintly through a gray mask of alkali. Ring Partridge was smaller, his narrow shoulders stooped in their horsehide vest, his sun-squinted eyes smoldering with an old hatred.

Upon Wolffe's advice, Sheridan had foreclosed on the long overdue notes of both these men, earlier in the year. Seeing the unveiled hostility in their faces, he knew an impulse to try and explain how little contact he'd had with the business of the Double Bit. Then he shrugged it away, knowing how useless apology was now.

"I never thought I'd see you riding with Salt River," Partridge said acidly, after they had taken Gillette into the house and come back outdoors.

Forge put a rope-gnarled hand on Partridge's arm. "Never mind, Ring. What happened out there, Sheridan?"

"Somebody's put bob wire around Rabbit Sink," Sheridan said. "When we tried to drive the beef through, they started shooting. Pa got hit and the cattle stampeded. They scattered out into the badlands north of the sink. Sandoval and his hands are out there trying to round them up. I don't think they'll have much luck."

"What now?" Partridge asked.

"The doctor, first. I'm riding as soon as I get a fresh horse."

Partridge frowned intensely. "Can't that Indian woman fix Pa up? I've seen her heal a man I thought was dead."

"Partridge is right," Forge said. "The doctor'll come out here. He's decent at the bottom. But he's a Tarrant man, and he'll talk. It's liable to break us up for good if word gets around how bad off Pa Gillette is. He was the driving force behind our bunch. It was bad enough when you foreclosed on him. A lot of borderline men thought we were finished then and went over to Tarrant."

"Tarrant's working like hell to get enough signatures on that recall petition, but he hasn't got fifty-one percent yet," Partridge said. "If we can only hang on till Mayor Prince gets the franchise voted through, we'll be safe. If it gets out that Pa's been hit this bad now, enough men like Sid Bouley and Wirt Peters are going over to Tarrant to give him that fifty-one percent."

Sheridan stared bleakly at the ground. "By the looks of that wire around Rabbit Sink, Bouley's already gone over." He shook his head. "Pa's hit bad. I hate to leave him without a doctor. If he died now . . ."

He broke off as Asa came to the door. The boy's eyes were like holes burned through the dust-caked mask of his gaunt face. Cameron followed him out, rubbing awkwardly at his rawhide britches. The five men stood in uncomfortable silence, trying furtively to find the answer to this in each other's eyes.

Finally Estelle came to the door, staring at them with a plea in her great blue eyes. She knew how things stood, and must have realized what they had been talking about. Finally she spoke, her voice pinched and trembling.

"I think the bullet's still in him. The Indian woman can't handle something like that. All she knows is poultices and herbs. It's so hard for him to breathe . . ."

She trailed off, circling them with her frightened eyes, and it dragged Forge's great shoulders down in defeat. "I guess you're right. I guess we better go for the doctor."

"This doesn't have to mean the end," Sheridan said. "If Tarrant wants to put the pressure on, we can, too. He's depending on the turncoats in our party to make up the rest of his votes on that recall petition. What's to stop us from seeing that they don't vote? Call a meeting. Find out just where everybody stands. Take the doubtful ones out in the badlands if you have to. Hold 'em there till Prince can get that franchise through. You'll have a shipping point in Apache Wells then. Tarrant can't stop your drives by blocking off the water holes."

A deep wonderment filled Forge's eyes, but then he shook his head. "If they come here, they'll know that Pa . . ."

"Choose a new leader. Admit Pa's hurt. What's wrong with Sandoval? He's got enough guts to string on a fence and he's the smartest one among you."

Partridge shook his head. "A lot of the men wouldn't take orders from an Indian." As if moved by the same idea, both Partridge and Forge looked at Asa. "How about you?" Partridge said. "The Gillette name'll still have a lot of pull."

Sheridan knew a disappointment, doubting the boy's ability. It must have shown in his face, for Asa turned defiantly to him. "It was your idea. Don't tell me you're backing out of it now."

Sheridan said: "Why not make your nominations and let them put it to a vote?"

Forge shook his head. "We can't do it that way. The vote would be too divided. It'd only leave things in a mess. We've got to have a leader when the men get here. I think they'd accept Asa. It's natural for him to step into his father's place."

"I'll make 'em accept me," Asa said. The flushed excitement in his face made it look even wilder. "We might as well start right now. Sheridan, you ride for the doctor. The rest of you each pick a section and round up all the Salt Rivers you can. Meeting'll be here, tonight at eight."

Partridge and Forge nodded and moved to their horses. Wearily Sheridan went to his animal and started leading it down to the corral. He was around the corner of the house when Estelle caught up with him. She walked beside him, looking up into his face, strain drawing at the corners of her eyes and mouth.

"I don't know how we'll ever thank you for saving Pa's life," she said. They were by the corral now, and he halted the horse, looking down at her.

"Don't you?" he asked.

217

She gazed, wide-eyed, into his face, so close the scent of her made him giddy. Her mouth parted, till the lower lip took on a pouting ripeness. He let the reins drop from his hands, and found his arms slipping about her. She came to him, and he bent his head to taste that ripeness. When it was over, she drew her head back, eyes large and dark with wonder.

"You've kissed me before," she whispered. "But never like that."

He rode after that. He saddled up while the girl stood outside the corral watching him, and left her there in the dusky compound. But all the way into Apache Wells she would not leave his mind. He had been unable to explore any further what had happened to them. Perhaps it was too new, too surprising.

In the past, he had courted her as gaily, as lightheartedly as he had courted a dozen other girls at the same time, with no serious intention toward any of them. Suddenly it was different. So different it shook him. It made him realize that he had learned more about life and about himself in these last few weeks than he had learned in all the time before.

It was well into the night when he got back to Sandoval's with Doc Bennett. There was a blazing campfire in the compound outside the house, surrounded by the silhouettes of the Salt River men. The meeting had apparently been going on for some time. Estelle met the doctor at the door and disappeared inside with him, and Sheridan went tiredly over to the fire.

As he approached the men, some seated on logs, others standing in little knots, he saw that Asa and Forge stood in the center, listening to one of the men in the crowd speak. It was Samuel Fallon, one of the smallest operators in the bunch, a thin, stooped figure with a nasal voice.

"Tarrant's bought up a lot of those notes Sheridan used to hold. He's threatening to foreclose now unless I put my name on that recall petition. My wife's due for another baby. We ain't got no place to go. Time comes when a man's got to think of his family."

Blond-bearded Wirt Peters nodded grimly. "If I don't get my beef to Tempe this year, I'm through. Tarrant's promised me the use of the water they control along the route if I'll come into his wagon. After what happened to Sandoval, it seems to be the only way a man could reach Tempe."

"Then why don't you all just jump right in Tarrant's wagon?" Asa said sarcastically. "You stand here and whine about all the things Tarrant's doing. If you haven't got the guts to stick it out . . ."

Sheriff Cline caught his arm. "Wait a minute, Asa . . ."

Asa spun toward him. "Why should I listen to you? Tarrant must have you in the hollow of his hand, too."

Cline shook his head. "You know I didn't have anything to do with foreclosing on you. Nacho handled it while I was gone on that wild-goose chase to the south end of the county. The more I think of it the more I think Tarrant engineered it so that I'd be out of the way."

"Then Nacho must be Tarrant's man . . ."

"Nacho was only carrying out his duty."

"Duty, hell," Asa said. "Carrying out Tarrant's orders, you mean. And you knew it."

Asa tried to wheel back, but Cline caught his arm again. "That's not true . . ."

"Take your hands off me!" Asa's voice left him like a whip, and he flung his arm out, tearing Cline's grip off and knocking the man backward. Cline tripped over the log behind them and fell heavily. He rolled to hands and knees, rising, his heavy face sallow with anger.

"You shouldn't 'a' done that," he said.

"Why not?" Asa's face held a whipped look. "I'm sick of you yellow-bellies whining about Tarrant when half of you are with him anyway."

A pucker of muscle ran through Cline's face and he seemed unable to check the little forward jerk of his body. Then Prince was between them, holding up his hands.

"Take it easy now, both of you. We can't fight among ourselves this way."

There was a tense silence, as Asa and Cline faced each other across the mayor's shoulder, their bodies stiff with anger. Then Fallon shook his head defeatedly.

"When you called this meeting, I thought you had something to offer for the men that was caught in the middle. It looks like all you want to do is scrap among yourselves."

Sheridan lifted his voice from the fringe of the crowd. "We do have something to offer."

Fallon turned suspicious eyes on him. "You and Wirt Peters both used to be Tarrant men. How do we know you still ain't? There ain't nothing left of the Salt River bunch. With Pa out of it, we're through. We might as well admit it."

There was a grumble of assent from half a dozen men, and they began moving away. Sheridan started to speak again, then subsided. He saw that a few were still remaining, eyeing him with a reserved expectancy. He realized they had achieved their purpose despite Asa's mistakes. The ones who remained now could certainly be counted on to stick. Wirt Peters was one of them, scratching at his stubby blond beard.

"What is this you have to offer?" he asked. "Seems to me it's a losing fight. Tarrant's trying for that recall on the basis that Prince took a bribe from the railroad to push the franchise through. If that's true, we haven't got a leg to stand on."

"You know it isn't true," Sheridan said. "Tarrant has Council-man Lewis under his thumb. Lewis claimed he overheard the division superintendent offer Prince a cut of the freight rates if Prince saw that the franchise went through. But Lewis has already served time on a perjury count down in Tempe. It's a trumped-up charge Tarrant couldn't possibly shove through until he has the Salt River bunch so whipped they won't fight it."

"What's that got to do with it?" Asa asked Peters. "We're here to . . ."

"You keep quiet, and let Sheridan do the talking," Prince told the boy. "You almost messed up things once tonight."

Asa started to react hotly, but Peters cut him off. "He's right, Asa. I think the ones that are left here will listen to Sheridan."

Asa subsided, tight-lipped, and Sheridan turned to the men.

"It's going to be a dirty game from here on in. We know the weak ones in our bunch now. Tarrant will hear about this meeting by tomorrow and will start pressing those men to sign the petition. We'll have to keep them from doing it. We'll pick them up one by one, hold them in the badlands till the franchise is voted through. Tarrant will lose his biggest stakes right there. Once we lick him on this franchise, we'll have a reason to hold on. A railroad in Apache Wells would make you all a dozen times bigger than you are now."

Peters began to chuckle. "Damn if I don't think we've got some brains in the Salt Rivers at last."

"You'll do it?" Sheridan asked.

Peters looked around at the others getting a nod from each man. "We'll do it," he said.

CHAPTER
SEVEN

It was getting on toward midnight, and the two Gillettes and Sheridan were too dog-tired for any more riding that night. The men remaining all bedded down at Sandoval's, planning to move into action the next morning. Sheridan slept with four others in the beargrass hut, awoke to the smell of coffee and the sound of sizzling bacon. Estelle was at the cook fire with Sandoval's wife, pouring coffee for the line of hungry men. Sheridan walked in, scratching at the red stubble on his lean jaw.

"How's Pa?" he asked Estelle.

Estelle brushed a wisp of honey-colored hair from her heat-flushed face, smiling at him. "Resting easy, Brian. Doc pulled the bullet out last night."

He looked around. "Where's Asa?"

She poured him coffee. "Mayor Prince and Cline went home last night. This morning Fallon brought a note to Asa from Prince. The mayor wanted to see Asa at his home."

"What about?"

"The note didn't say. It was urgent."

"Funny Fallon should bring it. He's one that walked out last night. Did you see him?"

"He came too early. Asa told me."

"We won't be able to wait for him," Sheridan said. "We're breaking up into groups and going to pick up the men we think might go over to Tarrant."

She caught his arm, looking up at him with a dark apprehension in her eyes. Then she shook it away, trying to smile.

"I was going to ask you to be careful. But I guess you can take care of yourself. You realize how you've changed in the last weeks, don't you, Brian?"

"Yes," he said, looking deeply into her eyes. "In more ways than you know."

The men worked out their plan of action after breakfast. Sheridan left with the others, but turned off alone toward Rabbit Sink. Sandoval would know by now whether he could round up his stampeded cattle in time to get them to Tempe. If he couldn't, they'd need his help. Sid Bouley was near Rabbit Sink and he was one of the doubtfuls. With Sandoval's help, Sheridan could pick him up. He took an extra saddle horse and traded off every hour so he could push fast.

It was a grueling ride, through the hottest part of the day, leaving his face an alkali-whitened mask, his clothes sweat-drenched and caked with dust. It was afternoon by the time he reached the sink and found the half-sheltered camp Sandoval had set up on the ridge north of the water. There was an ocotillo corral here jammed into a box-end gully, holding a pitiful handful of the Yaqui's cattle. Knowing he could not find Sandoval in the badlands north of the sink, Sheridan settled down to wait for the man's return.

Sandoval and his two Mexican hands came in near sundown, driving a quartet of gaunted cattle. Defeat stooped the Yaqui in the saddle. He gave Sheridan a listless salute, asking after Pa. Sheridan said Pa was all right, still staring at those cattle. Sandoval nodded heavily.

"I know what you think. At this rate, she take us all the year the cattle to round up, in this country. You're right. We're finished."

"Would you like to pay Bouley off a little?" Sheridan asked.

Sandoval reached thoughtfully for the *hojas* in the pouch at his belt, building himself a cigarette. "I know Rabbit Sink she belong to Bouley. But Juan something funny tell me. Some of the *hombres* who shot at us also rode down on the cattle to help stampede them that night, as you know. Juan say a good look he gets at one. It is Latigo. Riding one of your steel-dusts."

Sheridan felt the surprise of that pull his head up. "Latigo?" The word left him in a whisper.

Sandoval nodded, striking a spark with his flint and steel to light the cigarette. Sheridan shook his head. He supposed he shouldn't be surprised. It wasn't illogical that Latigo should go to work for Tarrant. And yet something about it started an insidious, indefinable suspicion working through his head.

Before he could speak again, they heard the pound of a hard-driven horse coming up the gully. Ring Partridge rode it, the wind whipping his greasy hat brim into sun-squinted eyes. He led another animal, and pulled the two sweat-channeled beasts up before the

225

half-sheltered camp. He had to speak loudly over the gusty roar of their breathing.

"I hoped I'd catch you before you left here," he panted. "Things have blowed up in our face, Sheridan. Asa's gone and murdered Sheriff Cline."

Sheridan felt the blood drain from his cheeks. His weight settled in a sodden way, like a man recovering from one blow and setting himself against the next.

"Let's have the rest of it," he said at last.

"You'd sent me and Forge to get George Purdy. Purdy's wife said he'd gone into Apache Wells. We hoped to catch him before he reached town. We hit Apache Wells without finding him. There was a big crowd in front of the jail. Nacho and Harv Rich had just brought in Cline's dead body, along with Asa. They claimed they came across Asa and the sheriff fighting on Look-Out Trail, and saw Asa kill Cline."

Sheridan's frown squinted his eyes almost shut. "What was Cline doing on Look-Out Trail?"

"Nacho said Cline had a tip this morning that the Apache Kid had been seen in Skeleton Cañon. Neither of his deputies had checked in, so he left word for them to follow him and meet him at the head of Look-Out Trail. Both Nacho and Harv Rich reached the office about a half hour after Cline had left and took out after him."

Sheridan was still frowning deeply. "And Fallon brought a note to Asa this morning, and Look-Out Trail is the closest route from Sandoval's to the mayor's house."

Sandoval was staring at him. "Something smells bad?"

"As Partridge said, this sure blows things up in our faces," Sheridan muttered. "The Gillette name still meant a lot to the Salt River men, no matter how close Asa came to botching things last night. This will kick a helluva lot of sand out of what men remain to us. It couldn't have been better for Tarrant if it had been planned."

"You think maybe it was planned?" Partridge said.

"Doesn't it seem like an awful big coincidence that Asa and Cline should hit Look-Out Trail at the same time?" Sheridan said. He shook his head. "Whatever happened, Asa's going to need the best lawyer we can get."

The beginnings of understanding built a frown into Sandoval's sun-blackened face. "Who are you think of, *amigo?*"

"I guess you know," Sheridan said, and then looked at the man almost defiantly. "It's worth a try, isn't it?"

CHAPTER
EIGHT

They spent that night in the Rabbit Sink camp. The need for hurry was gone now. What had happened completely ruined their plans. Sheriff Cline had been too well loved. By being aligned with the Salt Rivers, and thus with the killing, the mayor automatically lost any influence he might have had over the council that would have swung the franchise vote to the Salt River bunch's favor.

Despite the defeat oppressing Sheridan, he knew he still had to fight for Asa. It didn't matter that Asa had opposed him for so long. It was bound up deeply with Sheridan's feeling for Estelle. Asa was her brother, and, if he failed Asa, he would be failing Estelle, too. It was like stirring at ashes to find a new flame when the fire had already gone out, but his feeling for Estelle still drove him to it.

They parted the next morning, the other men heading back to Sandoval's, Sheridan taking a game trail through the badlands till he hit the Tempe Road, turning eastward along this to Apache Wells. As he traveled, it struck him how little all this riding affected him now. He sat easily in the saddle, no longer aware of the gall sores, the constant aching of muscle and sinew

228

that had plagued him so those first weeks of the roundup. His face was no longer red and raw from the sun and wind — it had been burned to a deep mahogany color. Even his senses seemed keener. He felt more acutely aware of everything that went on about him. It was like stepping into a new life, and despite his deep depression he felt a certain grim triumph in it.

In mid-afternoon he reached town. There was a little knot of men lounging in the shade of the wooden overhang before the Black Jack, but none hailed him. He passed the Mercantile, touching his hat brim in ironic salute to the pudgy figure in the doorway. Jess Miller turned back inside almost furtively.

Before the adobe jail was another group of men standing around Nacho, who sat tilted back in a chair against the wall, making a cigarette. They watched narrowly as Sheridan dismounted, moving toward the door. Nacho rose swiftly, placing himself before Sheridan.

"Nobody goes in there. Court order."

"Show me the order."

Nacho began to leer. "Old Double Bit, he's getting tough."

"Show me the order, Nacho, or get out of my way."

For a moment, the leer faded. Then it came again, and Nacho poked a sly finger against Sheridan's stomach. His brows rose, and he pursed his lips.

"Living thin's put ridges in your belly," he said. Then the leer returned. "It takes more than that to make guts, *amigo.*"

229

"If you don't get out of my way, we'll see about that," Sheridan said.

Nacho spread his boots a little. There was a sighing sound from the crowd. Sheridan felt the kink of nerves through his body. Before he could move, a tall, white-headed man in a frock coat parted the knot of men with the tip of his gold-headed cane.

"Mister Sheridan has a perfect right to see the prisoner, Nacho," he said. "You're taking your duties a little too seriously, I believe. You're not sheriff yet, you know."

Sheridan half wheeled to see that it was Judge Parrish, the circuit judge from Tempe who held district court in Apache Wells and other outlying towns four times a year.

"Thanks, Judge," Sheridan said. "How long can I have?"

"Fifteen minutes should be sufficient," Parrish said. "Step aside, Nacho."

Reluctantly the half-breed complied. Sheridan moved through the front office hung with faded Wanted posters and a rack of guns, and into the crude cell-block. One of the town drunks was snoring in the first cell. Asa stood in the second, hands clenched around the bars of the door. He did not try to hide his surprise.

"You're the last one I'd expect here," he said.

"You've got to quit fighting me, Asa," Sheridan said. "This thing has about finished the Salt River bunch, but we're still going to do everything in our power to help you." He paused, staring into the boy's haggard face. "Did you do it, Asa?" he asked simply.

230

Asa ran a thin hand through his unruly hair, red-rimmed eyes meeting Sheridan's in angry desperation. "No. I didn't, Sheridan, I swear I didn't. I was riding through Skeleton Cañon on my way to Prince's. I heard a shot. I got off my horse and went on foot through the rocks with my rifle. I came on Cline's body. That's where Nacho and Harv Rich found me."

"What about the note from Prince?"

"The mayor said he never wrote any such note."

"Where is it now?"

"I guess it was lost in the struggle. I put up a fight to keep Nacho and Rich from taking me in. When we reached town, the note wasn't in my pocket."

Sheridan shook his head. "That was our only evidence. If it wasn't Prince's handwriting, it could have been proved. Now all we have is your word that you got a note from Fallon."

"That's just it. Fallon's claiming he never brought me a note. I can't even prove that. Nobody saw him when he brought it that morning."

"It's all tied up," Sheridan said. "Fallon walked out on us at the meeting. He could well have gone to Tarrant that night. Harv Rich is a Tarrant man, and I suppose Nacho is, too."

"If they set it up, they did a neat job," Asa said. "They got Cline and me out of the way in one blow, and there isn't a thing we can prove."

Sheridan tried to make his smile reassuring. "Hang on, Asa. If it's humanly possible, we'll get you out of here."

All the hot bitterness was gone from Asa's eyes. "Thanks, Brian," he said. "I guess we've all misjudged you. Me most of all. If it'll do any good now, will you shake hands?"

They clasped hands through the bars, and no more words were necessary. Sheridan wheeled and walked out. He ignored the group at the door, tipped his hat to Judge Parrish, and walked on up the street to Wolffe's office. The door was locked. He went back down the rickety stairs and saw the banker's kid watching him owlishly from an alley. He found out from the boy that Wolffe might be found at the Double Bit. Sheridan stepped into the saddle again and with relief left the hostility of the town behind.

He thought the first sight of the ranch would hurt — the myriad windows flashing in the coppery glow of the sun, the barns and corrals backed up into the mist-purple foothills. But somehow he was filled with no hurt, no sense of loss. It was as if he had given it up to gain something infinitely better. His horse needed watering so he rode it on around behind the house to the trough by the first corral. He let it drink, and then hitched it to the fence and walked back to the house.

As he went around in front, he saw a man walking to intercept him from the barns. It was Latigo, and the man reached the porch before Sheridan. He went up a couple of steps and turned, thumbs tucked into the waistband of his Levi's, eyes measuring Sheridan insolently.

"Is Wolffe here?" Sheridan asked.

"No."

"Dee told me he was."

"He ain't!"

"Who is?"

"Me."

Sheridan started up the steps. "I'll see for myself."

Latigo made a sharp shift to block his way. "No you won't. This ain't your house any more, Sheridan. If Wolffe was in, he wouldn't want to see you."

Sheridan stared up at him, seeing the thinly veiled contempt in the man's eyes.

"I'm going in, Latigo," he said.

Latigo's lips peeled back in a wolfish smile. "Like you took the steel-dust away from me in Apache Wells?"

Sheridan hung a moment longer, meeting the man's stare. Then he lunged upward at an angle, as if trying to get around one side of Latigo. The foreman shifted hard that way to block Sheridan.

Sheridan stopped at the last instant. It left Latigo plunging forward without anything to block. He tried to catch himself, but it was too late. His impetus had carried him down beside Sheridan at an angle.

Sheridan hit him across the side of the neck, jackknifing him and knocking him down on the steps and off his feet. The man rolled over into the compound and came to his hands and knees. Sheridan jumped down off the steps at him. Latigo came up off his hands and knees, throwing himself at Sheridan's mid-section.

Sheridan went right into him, slamming an uppercut into his face. The blow and the smashing force of Sheridan's body pitched Latigo over backward. He

233

flopped over in the dirt a second time, staring up at Sheridan with a mixture of dazed pain and surprise in his face.

"Where's all that jelly now, Latigo?" Sheridan panted.

With a guttural sound, Latigo switched around and scrambled to his feet. Sheridan rushed him. Latigo ducked his first blow, feinting at Sheridan's face. Sheridan threw up an arm to block it. The real blow hit Sheridan in the solar plexus.

He couldn't help doubling over in pain. He felt Latigo cup those hands behind his neck. Felt the man's weight shift to slam that knee into his face.

He jerked aside in the last instant and caught the knee and heaved.

It pitched Latigo over on his back again. The blow dazed him and he shook his head before he rose again. This time Sheridan lunged in as soon as Latigo gained his feet. Latigo blocked his first blow and counterpunched for the solar plexus again. This time it struck Sheridan in the ridged muscle of his belly. Six weeks ago it would have doubled him over anyway. Now he only grunted and struck back. The blow rocked Latigo's head. He feinted at Latigo's belly. The man hugged his arms in and left his face open. Sheridan hit him in the face again. Latigo went down so hard it knocked the air from him with a sick grunt.

He lay on his belly a long time before rolling over. He finally raised his head, trying to focus his eyes on Sheridan. His breathing had a broken sound.

234

"You'd better not get up again, Latigo," Sheridan said. "You're whipped and you know it."

Latigo hung his head, spitting blood into the dirt. "Damn you," he said. The words seemed torn from him with great effort. "Damn you."

Sheridan waited till he was sure the man would not get up, and then turned to go in the house. Arleen stood on the porch. There was a flushed look to her face, an avid excitement shining in her eyes.

"Brian," she said huskily. "You're wonderful."

He was still breathing heavily, the sweat oiling his face, and he stood there a moment, regarding her cool beauty. She was in a velvet riding habit, its long skirt cut to accent her reed-slim waist. The cock feather sweeping over one shoulder from her perky hat was as scarlet as her lips. Despite the stunning impact of it there was something calculated about the whole effect. He wondered why he had never seen that before.

She came down the steps, lips parted, staring at the weathered hardness of his face. She put a hand almost hesitantly on his arm, feeling its lean muscle.

"How you've changed," she almost whispered. "I wouldn't believe it."

"I came to see George," he said.

Her eyes darkened, and she pouted. "Why George?"

He frowned at her. "You and he been fighting again?"

"Do we ever stop?" she said impatiently. "He didn't think it was fitting that we move out here. He said the rich living would get us. All he wants is that little hole of an office and those towsack clothes . . ."

"You're living here now?"

The sharp tone of Sheridan's voice brought her up. Something fluttered through her eyes. "It was some complicated deal of George's with Hadley and those Eastern architects. They couldn't do anything with the house even if they did get it back. George gave them a good price on the cattle if they'd turn their notes over to Hadley, and then he gave some of the land to Hadley or something. I don't understand how it worked . . ."

"If I know you, I think you do understand how it worked," Sheridan said, looking down at her. "I think you were behind the whole thing."

She brought herself closer, looking up into his face with that old breathlessness in her voice. "Not the details, Brian, you know that. I admit I influenced George. Somebody had to have the house, didn't they? It was such a white elephant. Why not us? Here we've scraped and done without and lived thin for so long and a chance like this came along . . ."

"Like a bunch of vultures," he said.

Her eyed widened, hurt. "Don't say that, Brian. You know it isn't like that. If I had my way, we'd have turned the house right back to you and you'd be back in it throwing those wonderful parties. But it was there, and nobody wanted it, and all George had to do was manipulate a few things . . ."

He couldn't help smiling ruefully. "You always wanted to live this way so bad, didn't you?"

"There" — she was smiling, too — "you don't blame me. I can see it. You understand."

"No." He shook his head slowly. "I don't blame you, Arleen." He studied her a moment. "But I still want to see George."

With an impatient sound, she turned and led him inside. Going through the door, he took a last glance at Latigo, only now getting up. They walked across the immense parlor and down the hall to the study. Without knocking, Arleen opened the door.

Wolffe was bent over some papers on the desk, and raised his head in surprise. The lines of his strong-framed face deepened as he saw Sheridan, and he came slowly to his feet. For a moment, the humorless withdrawal on his face held no welcome. Then he moved around the desk, a puzzlement growing on his face as he studied Sheridan.

"You look like a different man," he said.

"He is a different man," Arleen told her brother.

"I'll be brief, George," Sheridan said. "I've come to ask a favor. You know what's happened to Asa. I don't think he did the murder. I want you to defend him."

Surprise was in Wolffe's frown. Then he shook his head. "That wouldn't be any good, Sheridan. I think he did do the murder. All the evidence points that way."

"If you had evidence proving he didn't do it, would you defend him?"

A strange look tightened Wolffe's face. "You have evidence?"

"If I could get it . . ."

"Now you're talking supposition. I can't defend him on that."

"I'm talking friendship, George. For my sake, for the sake of what we once had, will you defend Asa?"

Wolffe spread his hands. "How can I? Without proof . . ."

"Give me a chance to get the proof."

"Where?"

"I don't know. You're a lawyer. I'm asking for your help, George. I'm asking you to defend him and to help us save an innocent man."

"I would if I thought he was innocent."

"You're saying you won't do it?"

Wolffe's eyes burned into Sheridan's for a moment, then he nodded. "That's what I'm saying."

Arleen went impulsively to her brother, catching his arm. "George, hadn't you better think it over . . . ?"

He threw her hand off, anger hot in his eyes. "Don't start your endless wheedling again. I got the house for you, didn't I?"

She flushed hotly. "George . . ."

"Be quiet, Arleen, and stay out of this. Haven't you caused enough trouble already?"

She stepped back, trembling with anger. "You'll be sorry for that, George. You'll see the day when you wish you'd listened to me."

Before he could answer, there was the tramp of boots from the living room and somebody hailed Wolffe. He looked at Sheridan, and Sheridan said: "That's your final answer?"

"My final answer, Brian."

Sheridan stared bleakly at him, saying finally: "I'll go out the back way. My horse is at the watering-trough."

238

He turned to go down the hall toward the rear door. Opening it and stepping through, he half turned to close it behind him. He saw Wolffe's figure blocked out against the other end of the passageway, just going into the living room, and heard Ford Tarrant's voice, rough with worry.

"Hadley's kid said Sheridan was coming out this way. You didn't . . . ?"

"No, I didn't," Wolffe said. "He asked me to defend Asa. I refused."

"Good, George. Good. I didn't want anything to go wrong at the last minute. If we can convict Asa of this murder, it will cook the Salt River bunch for good. Fallon and Bouley and half a dozen others have hopped over to our side like scared rabbits. Their names just about constitute the fifty-one percent."

Sheridan frowned, on the point of closing the door. Naturally Tarrant wouldn't want Wolffe to take the case. But it sounded like something more than that. An arrangement? He stepped back inside, closing the door loudly enough so that Wolffe would hear it. Then he stood there, hidden from the hall by an alcove.

Tarrant was still talking. "We've already put in for an emergency sheriff's election along with this recall. You agreed that Nacho would be our man. Now Latigo's telling all over town that he's going to be sheriff . . ."

"And he's right," Wolffe said angrily. "Just because you've had tabs on Nacho doesn't make him fit for a job like that. Get him full of that mescal and there's no telling what he'll do."

"Latigo's too insolent and hot-headed," Tarrant told Wolffe. "Nobody likes him in town. He never would take orders."

"He'll take orders from me."

"That's what I thought." Tarrant's voice was strained. "Then every man in office except me will belong to you, won't he? Councilman Lewis and Sheriff Latigo and . . ."

"What's the matter?" Wolffe asked sardonically. "Afraid I'll pinch you off?"

"I know damn' well you will. Just like you pinched off Sheridan when he wasn't any use to you any more."

As Tarrant said this, Sheridan stepped out into the hall and moved toward the living room. The study was empty, and he realized Arleen must be in the front, too. He could see none of them, but could still hear Tarrant's voice, rising from anger to a sort of hysteria.

"It's funny. Sheridan thought Casket was my man. You had Casket working on him for years."

"Shut up, Ford!"

"I will not." Tarrant's voice grew shrill. "I know how you work, Wolffe. Think I've been cultivating Hadley for my health? He's scared you'll pinch him off, too, and he's been squealing. How he helped you siphon off a big chunk of every Double Bit check that went through his bank. How you overcharged Brian for everything he bought, and pocketed the difference. That business about the deposit slips and the false accounts and everything else . . ."

"Damn you!" Wolffe shouted.

Sheridan stepped into the living room just in time to see him smash Tarrant across the face with a back-hand blow. It knocked Tarrant back against a tall jardinière. It tumbled over, crashing to bits on the floor, and Tarrant fell after it.

The motion had wheeled Wolffe around till he saw Sheridan, standing just inside the door. Wolffe settled back, the surprise fleeing swiftly from his eyes, leaving only unrelenting defiance. Sheridan stared at him, unable to feel anger in this moment of revelation. There was nothing but sick emptiness at the pit of him.

"I thought you'd gone, Brian," Wolffe said thinly.

"You, George?" Sheridan said in a dead voice. "All the time."

"I'm sorry you overheard," Wolffe said. Then he shrugged. "I guess it would have come out sooner or later anyway."

"Why, George? You could have become rich off the retainer I paid you alone."

"Rich? Chicken feed like that? What kind of man did you think I was? I licked boots long enough. I bowed and scraped and went without, till I had a bellyful. You didn't think I'd stand by and see a fool throw away the biggest ranch in Arizona? What do you know about riches? You and Tarrant were the biggest men in the county, but you were pikers. You're going to see a different Double Bit come out of this." Wolffe's voice rose higher. A flush filled his face. "It'll be bigger than you could ever dream of. Not just Apache Wells or Gila County. There's bigger game than that. This is just the start and the end is so far out of your sight you don't even dream of it . . ."

Sheridan stared at the feverish excitement flushing his face. He understood some of the burning intensity in Wolffe's eyes now. He should have realized Arleen was but a pale imitation of her brother. In her it was merely a love of riches for the surface glitter they could buy. In Wolffe it was a need for power.

"I guess I should have seen it a long time ago, shouldn't I?" Sheridan said. "You always did love to control men, push them around like you'd play a game of chess. You were like a schoolteacher with me. I couldn't make a move without your advice. Everything that's happened here has come from the way you've manipulated men. You need power like another man needs a woman."

"And now I've got it," Wolffe said harshly, sending half a glance to Tarrant, who was standing amid the ruins of the jardinière. "And what are you going to do about it?"

"Maybe you'll find out sooner than you think, George," Sheridan said softly.

CHAPTER
NINE

Sheridan got back to Sandoval's near midnight, but they were all waiting up for him. Estelle immediately began to heat something for him to eat, and Juan put his horse up, while Cameron and Sandoval and Pancho gathered before the stove in the low-roofed kitchen to hear what Sheridan had found out. He saw the surprise fill their faces as he told them of Wolffe, and saw that fade into deep defeat.

"I'm not surprised about Wolffe," Estelle said. "He never lived like a normal person. Seven days a week cooped up with those law books of his."

Sheridan shook his head dismally. "In a way, you can't blame him. The kind of boyhood he had would twist anybody."

"Not that much," Estelle said. "I think he'd be this way no matter how he grew up. Those burning eyes. I don't think I've ever seen him smile."

"Some men want women. Some want money. Some want power," Sandoval said. "Is no explaining. What now, Brian? Is it over?"

Sheridan accepted the plate of beef and beans Estelle handed him, dropping wearily onto one of the crude benches at the table.

"We can't just give up," he said. "I'm convinced Asa didn't kill Cline. If we had time, we might turn up some kind of proof that Asa was innocent, some clue, anything. But we don't have time. The trial's set for next Saturday and they have an air-tight case."

"You're right," Cameron said dourly. "Asa was seen quarreling with Cline by a dozen men."

"There's just one thing we've got to work with, as I see it," Sheridan said. "Wolffe has played every man off against the other till none of them trust him. Tarrant especially. I saw them fighting this afternoon and a lot came out. I think if we could get them mad enough at each other, the whole thing might bust apart."

"But how would that be evidence to free Asa?" Estelle asked.

"I don't know. I've got something in my mind about Judge Parrish. Nobody's got any strings on him here. I think he's a man to be trusted. If only he could be there when Wolffe and Tarrant start flying at each other."

"They wouldn't be fools enough to say anything in front of him."

"You can't tell what would happen if you got 'em mad enough . . . and if they didn't know the judge was there."

"That's crazy," Estelle said. "How can you gamble with Asa's life on such a flimsy idea?"

Sheridan looked up sharply. "The time's come for gambling. We've only got a few days left. Whatever we do, we've got to do it fast. We haven't a shred of evidence for the defense. Can you think of anything better?"

Estelle colored, dropping her eyes to the floor. "I'm sorry, Brian. I guess we're all jumpy."

"I think Brian he's right," Sandoval murmured. "Where we start, *amigo?*"

"By putting the pressure on Tarrant," Sheridan said.

They started that next morning. Sheridan wrote the letter to Tarrant, asking the man to come to the Double Bit, saying it was urgent, signing it with George Wolffe's name. Sheridan had seen enough of Wolffe's writing to make a fair imitation of the man's strong hand, and did not think Tarrant would question it too closely.

Then Sheridan rode to Wirt Peters. He was convinced of the man's loyalty, even though Peters had once worked for Tarrant. That fact was what made him useful. Tarrant had undoubtedly been waiting for Peters to desert the Salt Rivers and come back to him, and would find nothing questionable when he did so. When Peters heard Sheridan's plan, he agreed to take the letter to Tarrant, saying that Wolffe had persuaded him to come back on their side.

After that, Cameron and Sandoval and Sheridan went up to Skeleton Cañon to wait. Sheridan put the two men high on the rimrock with their rifles, telling them to take a couple of shots at Tarrant without actually hitting him. Then Sheridan took up a position back in one of the spur cañons.

The sun burned its way across the sky and the shadows lengthened in the cañon till its farther side was shrouded in gloom. This was the nearest route between Tarrant's and the Double Bit, but after a while

Sheridan began to wonder if something had slipped up. He saw a furtive motion up there and knew Cameron and Sandoval would be getting impatient. Then he heard the *clatter* of hoofs on shale far down the cañon. He tightened his cinch and stepped aboard the horse.

The first *crack* of a gun made the beast start and try to rear. He pulled it down, fighting to hold it in while the other shots filled the cañon with their deafening roar. Then he let the buckskin go, running headlong out into the main gorge.

He saw that Tarrant had been pitched off his hammer-headed mare, and was just rolling onto his hands and knees in the sand. A bullet kicked up sand a foot from him and he took a sprawling dive for the cover of boulders. The buckskin was frightened enough by all the bedlam so that Sheridan could make his struggle to stop it look real. As he raced by, Tarrant came up from behind the rocks, snapping a shot at him.

Sheridan saw a soft spot in the sand and took a dive. There was a new racket of gunfire from up on the ridge as he hit, rolling through the sand, limp as an empty sack. He finally came over to his hands and knees and lunged for the rocks on the same side as Tarrant. Then he sprawled there, shouting at the man.

"What the hell are you shooting at me for? I'm not your bushwhacker." He saw Tarrant stare at him foolishly, then turn a look back up to the rimrock. The shots had ceased now. Sheridan crawled down behind the scattered boulders till he reached Tarrant. The man looked at him suspiciously.

"What are you doing here?"

"Riding to town," Sheridan said.

Tarrant was still holding his gun on Sheridan. "Your bunch got things a little crossed up, didn't they?"

"Crossed up, hell," Sheridan said disgustedly. "If we'd wanted to bushwhack you, I wouldn't be fool enough to go riding down here."

Flattened against the rock, Tarrant stared back up at the rim again. Sheridan could see the anger turning to confusion in his face.

"Funny," Sheridan said. "This is almost the same spot I was bushwhacked when I was coming out to the Gillettes that time. You and Wolffe had me convinced it was the Gillettes. It sure couldn't be them this time."

Tarrant turned back to him, the confusion becoming an ugly suspicion in his eyes now. "You didn't set this up?"

"Why should I?" Sheridan asked. "What good would it do me? I know you're not the leader of the Tarrant faction now. It was Wolffe behind everything."

"Everything?" Tarrant frowned up at the rimrock again.

"They're gone," Sheridan said. "You don't think they'd stick around after they missed like that, do you? What were you doing here anyway?"

Tarrant did not answer, apparently studying what harm he could cause by telling Sheridan. Finally he muttered: "Wolffe sent me a note to come out to the Double Bit. It was urgent."

"Seems like everybody's sending notes."

Tarrant looked at him sharply. "What do you mean?"

"Asa got a note that Prince wanted to see him, didn't he? It sure led him into a lot of trouble."

"Yes . . ." — Tarrant sagged against the rock, and Sheridan could see the ugly suspicion blossoming in the man's mind — "a lot of trouble."

"Who's going to be sheriff, Tarrant?"

Tarrant looked up sharply. "Nacho is."

Sheridan chuckled softly. "That isn't what Wolffe said in the last meeting at the old Archuleta place. He said he'd bring me word this Thursday night that Latigo was in for sure."

Tarrant's eyes narrowed. "The old Archuleta place?"

"He said you'd be there this evening," Sheridan went on, as if only half hearing him. "Why weren't you there the last time? Wolffe said you . . ."

Sheridan trailed off, letting his lips part faintly, as if he had finally seen the tension filling Tarrant's face, as if he had finally realized he had said too much. Tarrant grabbed his coat, voice strained.

"What are you talking about? Are you and Wolffe making a deal behind my back?"

"Take your hands off me, Tarrant."

The man closed his fist tighter, jerking at Sheridan. "Not till you tell me. What about the old Archuleta place . . . ?"

Sheridan grabbed his wrist and tore it free. The man tried to bring his gun around but Sheridan hit it with the flat of his hand, slapping it aside. At the same time he slammed Tarrant across the side of his head, knocking him into the sand. He rose and stepped over to the man, kicking the gun out of his hand before he could rise again.

"I thought you knew," he said, looking down at Tarrant. "If you haven't got sense enough to keep your own pot boiling, it isn't my fault."

With a disgusted sound, he turned and walked down the cañon after his horse. He knew a dozen ugly inferences of what he had said must be going through Tarrant's mind now. His sole hope was that he had planted the suspicion strongly enough to take Tarrant out to the old Archuleta place.

It took him half an hour to find his horse. Then he rode to the north end of the cañon and into the badlands to the Devil's Horse pasture, where he had arranged to meet Sandoval and Cameron. They were waiting impatiently for him. He told them how it had gone, and sent them into Apache Wells to get Judge Parrish. Then he rode on toward the Double Bit.

He was working on a narrowing margin of time. Everything depended upon his knowledge of Arleen's habits now. If only she still took that ride on Indian Summit every afternoon near sundown.

He reached the summit with a dying sun turning the sky crimson. He pushed his jaded horse through the great outcroppings of sandstone that made a labyrinth of the ridge, until he reached the hollow from which could be seen the desert below. Here he pulled up sharply.

Arleen stood beside a blood bay, a stunning figure in her scarlet habit. His first appearance had caused her to wheel, surprise on her wind-flushed face. That narrowed to calculation.

"Isn't this a little out of your way?" she asked.

He stepped off his horse, smiling ruefully. "I wasn't actually going to town. I guess I sort of hoped I'd find you up here."

Then he saw something else in her face beside the calculation. Her lips were pinched in, repressing some indefinable anger. He moved closer, seeing the red mark on her neck. She saw him looking at it and turned to hide it.

"Take a fall?" he said.

Her eyes drew thin. "No."

"Don't tell me . . . George . . . ?"

"Let's not talk about it," she said.

He moved in, catching her shoulders, turning her back. "You can tell me, Arleen. I saw you quarreling the other day. I knew you had your spats. I didn't know it was this bad."

Her lips tightened, as if she were making an effort to repress it, and then she gave a savage shake of her head. "He seems to get worse every day. The more he gets, the tighter he is with it. I thought I could teach him how to live when we were on top. But all he can think about is getting more. It seems like we're living thinner now than when we had nothing. It's like being in prison. He begrudges me every penny I spend. And not only the money. He's changing, Brian. It frightens me. He gets so violent whenever it comes up. Like hitting Tarrant the other day. I don't know . . ."

Sheridan studied her, seeing his chance in this. "Why don't you leave him?"

"Where would I go?"

"Where I'm going," he said. She looked up in surprise, and he went on. "It's all over for me, Arleen. The Salt Rivers are smashed."

"And Estelle?"

"Peaches and cream and sweetness and light. Just like you said."

He saw a flush of triumph break through her anger. "And you still want me, after all that's happened?"

"I realize you weren't to blame for what happened to me," he said. "What you wanted you were always honest about. If you took advantage of it after they'd smashed me, nobody could blame you. It was George who ruined me. I know that now. But he won't have it long, Arleen. We can leave this damned desert. New York. Paris. Everything you ever wanted."

She frowned. "What do you mean . . . he won't have it long?"

"He's built a house of cards. He pulled a dirty trick for every dollar he's got, and there are a dozen men just waiting to jump him. You could get back at him for all those grubbing years, could have everything he wouldn't give you. We've got something that will take it right out from under George."

"We?"

"You know who I mean."

"Tarrant?"

"Who else is big enough to pull George down?" Sheridan said. "I'm meeting him at the old Archuleta place tonight. He's got something that'll blow the whole thing sky high. All we need is some of those deposit slips George was using when he was juggling my accounts."

He saw anger start up in her eyes. She veiled it with a drop of her lashes. Now he could feel the old calculation rising up in her. Her anger at Wolffe, her frustration, had been genuine. But now she was acting again. He could feel it in the subtle alteration of her body, moving closer to him. Her voice was a cat's purr.

"Brian . . . how do I know you'll go through with it . . . ?"

He slid his arms about her, pulling her in hard, and kissed her. There was nothing in it for him. It was like ashes in his mouth. But he made it bold and brutal, bringing to bear all the new forces he had found in himself these last weeks. It must have moved her. She was trembling when it was over.

"You never kissed me that way before," she said.

Sheridan grinned faintly. "I never played for such high stakes before."

CHAPTER
TEN

After he left her, he pushed his horse to the hilt out toward the Archuleta place. He almost felt sorry for Arleen. She had agreed to get the deposit slips, and meet him. There had still been that strange new look in her eyes, a little awe of him, perhaps a little fear. But behind it lurked the calculation that would never leave her. And he knew the conflict that must be tearing her now.

He knew he had shaken the girl, had held out strong temptations to her. But always before, no matter how she and Wolffe had fought, her loyalty to him had been the uppermost thing. Even in the old days, when she had tried to mold Sheridan to her own desires, she had not done so unless they coincided with her brother's desires.

Sheridan cut through Skeleton Cañon, its rock walls rising in jagged monoliths against a ghostly sky. At its north end he met Cameron and Sandoval, holding fretting horses in a spur cañon. With them was Judge Parrish. When the judge saw who Sheridan was, he let out suppressed anger in a righteous burst.

"What in the hell do you hope to gain by this . . . ?"

"No time to talk now, Judge. I'm hoping you'll hear some evidence that wouldn't have been introduced in court. If you can still convict Asa of murder after what you hear tonight, I'll stand trial alongside of him."

Parrish stared in amazement. Sheridan turned to Sandoval, who still held a gun on the judge.

"We'll go through the Devil's Horse pasture. I want you to watch for fresh sign as we go in."

They left the cañon and struck the badlands, all black lava and sun-twisted earth and scattered boulders. Sandoval had been tracking in this country all his life, and even in the moonlight Sheridan could trust him to spot the sign. They were about a mile from the Archuleta place when the Yaqui pulled his horse in sharply and stepped off. He squatted a moment over a strip of sandstone.

"One horse. Heavy ridden. 'Bout hour ago."

"That's Tarrant," Sheridan said. "He always was hard on his animals. I don't think he'll go down to the Archuleta place unless both Wolffe and I are there. He'll be watching from somewhere."

"And Wolffe won't go in unless both you and Tarrant he can see there," Sandoval said.

"That's it. Wolffe's too smart to be sucked in. He'll probably have Latigo with him. They'll scout around. And if Tarrant is still out here watching, either he'll pick up Wolffe, or Wolffe will pick up him. All that's left is the bait."

Sandoval frowned at him. "The bait?"

"I'll be down there where both of them can see me," Sheridan said. "Wolffe will want to know what Tarrant's doing here. Tarrant will want to know what Wolffe's doing. Neither of them will be able to tell the other. Neither of them will believe the other. Don't you think they'll come down to me sooner or later?"

Sandoval grabbed his arm. "*Amigo*, that is big chance . . ."

"The whole thing's been a big chance from the first. But it's all we've got left. Now, you've got to hold Parrish at a spot where Wolffe and Tarrant won't find you or see you. Yet it'll have to be near enough so you can see when Wolffe and Tarrant go down to the house. Those ridges to the north might be it. As soon as you see all of us down there, you come in."

Sheridan met the Yaqui's eyes, saw him nod, grinned at Parrish, and then turned his horse boldly on through the badlands trail. Tension crawled at his back as he neared the house, for he knew Tarrant was somewhere in the surrounding buttes, probably watching him now. But he felt half a triumph that he had sucked the man in this far.

The Archuleta place lay in a hollow, overlooked on all sides by buttes and mesas, an old Spanish colonial, built here in the times before Americans had seen the land. The adobe walls were fallen in, the roof had dropped its beams into the rooms. Sheridan spurred his animal right through a breach in the living room wall.

Moonlight came through the gaps in the roof to illuminate the great chamber, heaped with the rubble of collapsed walls. Sheridan hitched his horse and kicked together kindling from the rotting rafters and lit a fire in the center of the room. Then he sat on a fallen beam to wait.

Now all the doubts and apprehensions began to scrape his nerves. Had he misjudged Arleen tonight? Perhaps her loyalty to her brother would not override her anger with Wolffe this time. Perhaps she would not go to him with this. Perhaps she would really come with the deposit slips.

Sheridan realized he was sweating. There was a faint sound from somewhere outside. He fought to keep from turning.

Maybe if Wolffe came, the anger of the two men would break into shooting when they found each other out there. Sheridan shook his head. Wolffe would want to know what Tarrant had first.

Or maybe Tarrant wasn't convinced it had been Wolffe trying to bushwhack him in Skeleton Cañon. Maybe they would compare notes. Again Sheridan shook his head. He had seen them in their rage the other day. They had been in no shape to compare notes.

A voice broke out of the darkness suddenly, startling him.

"What the hell were you looking for?" Was that Wolffe? "Get in there along with him. And don't make a move, Brian. I've got you covered, too."

Sheridan had already stood up, but he kept his hand carefully away from his gun. In a moment Tarrant stepped through the breach, face white with frustrated anger. After him came George Wolffe, his Frontier Colt in one hand, Tarrant's six-gun jammed into his belt.

Sheridan realized it had happened as he had guessed it would. Wolffe had seen Sheridan down here in the light of the fire, had scouted a circle around the house to make sure it was no trap, and had found Tarrant.

Wolffe came over to Sheridan before he spoke, yanked Sheridan's gun from its holster, threw it far into the darkness.

"I hardly believed Arleen," he said in a voice strained with anger. "You were a fool to think she'd sell me out, Sheridan. As mad as she could ever get at me, when the chips are down, she wouldn't turn on me. She came straight to me with that pretty little story about you and Tarrant up here."

Tarrant stared at Wolffe, baffled surprise mingling with the anger in his face. "What are you talking about, George? You sent for Sheridan."

Latigo stepped through the breach and into the light, a smoldering hatred filling his half-lidded eyes as they settled on Sheridan. "Everything's clear outside," he told Wolffe. "I scouted all around and didn't find anybody."

Wolffe hardly seemed to hear him. "Don't try to twist this around, Ford," he told Tarrant. "What about those deposit slips? What can you add to them that would ruin me?"

"Deposit slips?" Tarrant snapped. "What's that got to do with it? You've been meeting Sheridan here and you can't deny it. Why else would he be waiting?"

"I haven't been here since I was a kid," Wolffe said.

"And I suppose you didn't have Latigo try to cut me down this afternoon."

Wolffe's eyes shuttled in surprise to Latigo. "Why would I want him to do that?" he asked sharply.

Tarrant's voice was shrill with frustrated rage. "For the same reason you had him cut down Cline."

"Asa killed Cline," Latigo snapped.

The words seemed squeezed from Tarrant by the force of his rage. "Don't be a fool. I was right there when you and Wolffe set it up and you know it. I even saw Wolffe write that note to . . ."

"Shut your driveling mouth!" Wolffe shouted, lunging forward to stop his words with a blow across the face that knocked Tarrant back into the wall.

Tarrant hung there a moment, stunned, barely keeping himself from falling. Then he gathered his body, wiping a sleeve across his bleeding lips. His face was white with rage.

"That's the last time you'll do that," he said. "You aren't going to squeeze me out, Wolffe. You made a bad mistake when you left it to Nacho to destroy the note they found on Asa. He didn't destroy it. He brought it to me. Maybe it reads like it came from Mayor Prince, maybe it's signed with his name. But any expert could prove it was your handwriting in a minute. You had Latigo kill Cline . . ."

Latigo lifted his gun sharply. "Damn you . . ."

Tarrant stiffened against the wall. "Kill me and that letter will be put into the hands of the court. It'll be proof enough to hang you both."

Wolffe settled back, his burning eyes moving to Sheridan for a moment. His lips grew thin as he must have realized there was no more use of pretense.

"Go ahead," he said acidly. "Why not tell Sheridan the whole thing, Ford? You've already spilled enough to finish us all. So I set it up to get both Cline and Asa out of the way in one stroke. The sheriff's office left open for one of our men and the new leader of the Salt River bunch smashed, all at once."

"And then me out of the way, leaving it all in your hands," Tarrant said in a thick voice. "Isn't it too bad you missed in Skeleton Cañon this afternoon?"

A puzzled look momentarily blocked the anger from Wolffe's face. "Skeleton Cañon?"

"Don't try to deny it. You sent me a letter just like you did Asa. You had Latigo waiting up on the rocks . . ."

Sandoval stepped into the firelight, gun in hand. "I think the judge he's heard enough. Don't do it, Wolffe!"

But Wolffe's response had been so automatic he could not stop it. He wheeled and fired all in an instant. The bullet knocked Sandoval backward even as Sandoval fired. Sandoval's bullet hit Wolffe hard, spinning him half around and dropping him to both knees. At the same time, Tarrant lunged for the fire. Sheridan jumped in to intercept him. Latigo had his gun out and threw down on Sheridan.

But Sandoval was holding himself up in the door frame, and he shot Latigo. The foreman made a mewing sound and doubled over and fell on his face. Tarrant reached the fire before Sheridan could get him, scattering the logs with one swinging kick. Sheridan caught him just beyond, knocking the man off balance with his charge.

They both pitched to the ground. Tarrant swung a wild haymaker that stunned Sheridan, and he lost contact with the man. He rolled over blindly, and then stopped as his senses returned.

He realized he was lying in darkness. The fire had been scattered and only a few coals remained, lying here and there across the floor. Their glowing perimeter of illumination only included Latigo, sprawled on his belly. Beyond him it was utterly black. One by one the coals winked out till there was no light at all.

There was no sound after that. And Sheridan knew why. Both he and Tarrant were unarmed. Sandoval knew that. The Yaqui was still alive, and he would have called out, unless he was afraid of drawing Wolffe's fire. The fact that Sandoval had not called out could only mean one thing. Wolffe was out there in that blackness somewhere, still alive.

Then Sheridan heard a faint stir off to his right. He guessed that was Tarrant. And he guessed the same thing was in Tarrant's mind as was in his. Latigo was wounded or dead out there, with a full gun. Sheridan knew Wolffe was only waiting for one of them to move. But he couldn't let Tarrant get that gun. He heard the faint stirring again. It seemed farther out from the wall. There was only one way. He rose to his feet and took a couple of lunging steps, and then went into a sprawling dive for the foreman.

There was a deafening blast of sound and the cherry flash of a gun before him. He felt the bullet hit his boot heel. Then he went into Latigo, clawing to stop himself on the man, and pawing for his gun. There was a second shot, the bullet *thudding* into the ground in front of his face. Dirt kicked into his mouth.

Gagging on it, he found the gun and yanked it from the man's hand, flinging it upward to fan it at the spot where those gun flashes had come from. He heard a grunt of pain. There was another gun flash, but it was pointed upward. He kept slapping the hammer till his gun was empty.

The echoes of the shots took a long time to die. The smell of black powder hung greasily in the air. Finally it was soundless again.

"All right, Chino," Sheridan said. "I got Wolffe, and Tarrant hasn't got a gun."

Sandoval sounded feeble. "Get some light. I got a bead on that breach in the wall, Tarrant. You'll be skylight if you try to go through."

Sheridan kicked together the logs again, got some kindling, lit a second fire. Its light showed Latigo and Wolffe sprawled out on the floor, both dead. Tarrant was on his feet, standing back against the wall. Cameron and the judge issued from the breach, supporting Sandoval between them.

"Don' treat me like baby," the Yaqui protested. "All I got she's little nick in the side."

Sheridan was staring at the judge, and Parrish nodded his head ruefully.

"Damnedest court I ever held, but what I heard tonight will sure free Asa. If you get another judge to sit on the case, I'll be a witness to this whole thing. If Tarrant has that letter in Wolffe's handwriting, it'll clinch the case."

"You won't get anything out of me," Tarrant said sullenly.

"What we heard tonight was enough to convict you of complicity in Cline's murder," Judge Parrish told him. "The most you can expect is the leniency they might give for the state's evidence that letter constitutes. You'd better play it smart, Tarrant."

"I don't think we need to worry about him," Sheridan said. "Can you ride with that wound, Chino?"

The Yaqui nodded. "I guess you got little girl to tell all about this, no?"

"She said she'd be waiting outside of town," Sheridan said.

She was. Honey-haired and big-eyed, with fear in her face, until she was sure he wasn't hurt. The judge and Cameron went on in with Sandoval and Tarrant, leaving Sheridan and the girl beneath the willows where she had been waiting so long for them. The shadows were so black he could hardly see her, and it was only their voices, husky and trembling with all the things they had to say.

"Maybe you can get part of the Double Bit back when it comes out how Wolffe cheated you," she said.

"I'm not worried much about that," he said. "What I found these last few weeks is worth more than any part of the Double Bit."

"What did you find?"

"Myself, for one thing. And more than that. You."

There was a catch in her voice. "When you were the biggest man in Apache Wells, you had a dozen girls."

"Now I've only got one. It's just you, from now on, Estelle. If you want it that way."

She lifted her lips for the kiss, her face shining with desire and fulfillment. All in one. "I do, Brian. From now on."